Icicles to Moonbeams

Christmas Eve Blessings

Sharon K Connell
Visit my website at www.authorsharonkconnell.com

Printed in the United States of America

First Printing: November 2019
KDP Publishing

ISBN-13 978-1-7329237-2-0

This book is dedicated to my Lord Jesus Christ who has given me the ability to write and guided me through the story.

Acknowledgements

My thanks to:

Arnold C. Hauswald, U.S. Army (Ret.) for your support and encouragement even during the late dinners, sleepless nights, and grumpy days of the creation of this first novella. You are the best man I know.

ACFW Scribes Critique Group

And the many members of the Christian Writers & Readers Facebook Group Forum for their encouragement. I am ever so grateful.

And now abideth faith, hope, charity, these three; but the greatest
of these is charity.

1 Corinthians 13:13

—KING JAMES AUTHORIZED VERSION

All Scripture used in this novella are taken from the King James
1611 Authorized Version

Icicles to Moonbeams

Christmas Eve Blessings

Sharon K Connell

Chapter One

A chill traveled through Alanna McCarthy as though icicles dripped down her spine. "How do I get over this pain?"

She pushed her bedroom window lace curtains aside and gazed out at the green and partially yellow leaves carpeting her front yard from one side to the other. Last night's storm sure had ravaged the trees and plants. Houston trees didn't usually lose so many leaves the first of September, not to mention several branches. But the damage matched her shattered heart. Since December twenty-second, the first day of winter last year, sharp pain like piercing icicles had replaced the warmth of Jake's love.

How could a healthy, vital man have a heart attack at such a young age? Ten years into their marriage. Tears sprang to Alanna's eyes—her usual ritual in the early morning when she rose from a fitful night's sleep. Too often, her mind replayed that horrible phone call. *"Mrs. McCarthy, I have some bad news. Your husband..."* She had to stop dwelling on it. Alanna breathed a bitter laugh. Like that would ever happen.

She pulled a tissue from the box on her nightstand and dabbed at her eyes. How appropriate for the weather to remind her so she could prepare herself for more heartache as she approached another winter of memories. He'd turned thirty the day before it happened, only two years older than she. Had they celebrated too much that day? She'd wanted to give him a birthday he'd never forget. But she was the one who would always remember.

Would she ever get over this depression?

The white curtains fell back across the window, and Alanna trudged across the thick carpet to the bathroom. She sighed. The house was so quiet. Why had they put off having children? They'd have filled her life in Jake's absence. Maybe they would have had two. She shook her head. Best not think about that either.

A disgusted huff came out of her. How could she be so callous, thinking of herself? If they'd had children, the kids would have no father. And how would she take care of them all alone? They'd be so young. Others had done it, but could she have managed? Surely not with the grief that engulfed her. How did people do it?

After a shower, she changed into a blue tailored suit and pale cream blouse. She sat on the antique desk chair Jake had given her two Christmases ago. It occupied a special place in the corner of the room next to her antique chifforobe he'd bought for her on their first Christmas. She'd always wanted one. The chair creaked as she moved, even with her light frame.

He'd bought her these shoes too. She stroked the soft leather of the blue one-inch heels in her hand and then slipped them on her feet. He'd been so good to her. Spoiled her, really.

Alanna heaved another heavy sigh and peered into the mirror over the six-drawer, lowboy, walnut dresser. She was too young to be a widow. "Oh, snap out of it, Alanna! Enough is enough. It's past time you got back into the real world."

Her shoulders slumped. She'd already tried. Time after time over the past months. The hole in her heart kept growing. Nothing...no one seemed to fill it. "Why can't I move on?"

And now this. Laid off from her job at North Houston Regional Hospital and three months before the holiday. *Another rotten Christmas.* She sniffled.

Two weeks' severance pay. *How generous.* Sarcasm was unbecoming, but she couldn't help herself. Cutbacks. How could they afford to cut back on employees when there were so many sick people at this time of the year?

She brushed her long blonde hair as if it were responsible for her problems. This year's flu epidemic alone should make the need for health care more crucial. They'd been shorthanded last year when Jake contracted the flu. If they hadn't been, he wouldn't have died. No doubt, the flu and its complications had taken a toll on his heart.

Alanna stopped torturing her hair and stared at the brush. She tugged at the strands she'd ripped out, tangled in the bristles. Blaming the hospital wasn't fair. It wasn't their fault he had complications. Nor that his heart wasn't able to cope. She dropped the brush to the dresser top. But he'd been so healthy. No one had ever diagnosed him with the heart problem that caused his death.

"Don't go there, Alanna. You'll upset yourself more."

But why lay off people now? Sure, she was a mere secretary to the nursing department. But they needed clerical assistance. Didn't they?

Big business, that's all it had become to the powers-that-be. Cutting back on the employees who had worked there long enough to make a decent living and doubling the work for those paid entry-level wages.

As she left the bedroom, she grimaced. Was she exaggerating? Maybe. Anyway, she had to find a new job. And good jobs had become scarce in Houston for her area of expertise. She'd thought clerical work would always be in high demand.

In the kitchen, Alanna poured herself a cup of coffee and dropped a slice of rye bread into the toaster. And what was with their telling her she had the least seniority at her pay level? She knew for a fact they gave a new hire the one open job she'd have been happy to fill. "But how does one compete with the best friend of the department supervisor?" Her brows puckered.

The toast popped, and she flipped it onto a waiting plate. "Ouch. Hot." Today she'd see what kind of jobs were out there. She lifted the plate and mug and plodded to the living room desk.

While she nibbled dry toast and sipped coffee, Alanna opened her computer and scanned employment sites. Should she go to an unemployment agency and let them find something for her? Not so sure. She'd heard horror stories from others about the places they sent applicants. Didn't matter what distance a person limited their job search to or the type of work they had listed. "What a mess I'm in."

Weeping made an encore appearance. "Oh, Jake, why did you have to leave me? We were so happy."

Alanna's cell rang. She wiped the tears from her eyes with the paper towel she'd grabbed for a napkin and picked up the phone from the edge of the desk. "No. Not Steve Brenner." He'd become a dreaded annoyance. She had no time for his nonsense.

After allowing the call to go to voice mail, Alanna placed her dirty dishes in the sink, rinsed them off, and loaded them into the dishwasher. No need to check the message. It would be the same one he always left, asking her out for dinner.

She glanced out the kitchen window. The backyard was as covered in leaves as the front. Bet the roads would be slick until they dried. Did the heavy rain flood the streets that usually do? Maybe she should avoid them altogether.

Alanna stepped into the foyer and swung a knitted shawl onto her shoulders. She picked up her briefcase armed with copies of her resume and a reference letter from her now-former boss. She took a deep breath and locked the door behind her. Her feet trudged over the wet stepping-stones to the driveway, and she slid into the driver's seat of her white Honda Civic.

She deposited her purse and briefcase on the passenger side floor, then ran her hand over the light blue, leather dashboard. What a wonderful birthday present this had been from Jake five years ago. She'd never had her own car before. The man had been so good to her. *Stop your blubbering.* She didn't want to forget Jake, just remember the good things without feeling the terrible loss...and move on. *Is that so much to ask, God?*

The cell rang. She reached for her purse, yanked it onto the passenger seat, and fumbled for the phone. She pulled it from the purse and checked the caller ID. Steve again. Alanna shoved the cell back into the bottom of her bag and started the engine. "Why can't that man leave me alone?" She'd told him over and over she wasn't ready to start seeing anyone. Yet, he continued to ask. "Who on earth gave him my number?" So far, no one had owned up to it.

Alanna backed out of the driveway and drove down the street. Steve had been pretty chummy with Alicia from Human Resources, but she wasn't supposed to give out personal information without the employee's consent. *Ha!* Since when did rules prevent people from doing things they shouldn't when there was an ulterior motive? But what would Alicia's have been? Oh, well. It didn't matter. It was done. He had the number and persisted in calling. She would simply persist in not answering until he got the message.

She should change her number, but it was such a hassle. Then she'd have to tell her sister why it was changed, which would cause an entirely different problem. No. Better to ignore the calls.

"Get your mind off him and onto your job hunt." She had her days free to search for a job since the hospital had immediately released everyone they laid off. *Forget about it, and get on with your life.* That's what she needed to do.

Alanna's hands grew clammy as she waited in front of a desk while the lady in Human Resources perused her resume and application. At least this time someone bothered to look at them instead of showing her where to drop the papers, to be reviewed later.

"Miss McCarthy, your work history is excellent, but you're overqualified for the position we have open." She wiped a stray curl from her forehead.

"But ma'am, I can do the work. Starting over in a new job doesn't bother me." She was so tired of hearing that phrase—the fifth time today.

"You seem to be a hard worker, and the reference letter from your last boss tells me you'd pour your entire work ethics into this job, but still."

Alanna glanced at the woman's name plaque on the desk. "Miss Gerrard, I really need the job, and entry-level for the position would be within the salary range I'd need to provide for myself."

The woman smiled at her, paper clipped Alanna's application to her resume and laid it in a tray at the corner of her desk. "We'll be in touch." She stood.

Alanna pressed her mouth shut to avoid saying any more. She didn't want to sound desperate. End of interview.

Half an hour later, she parked in her driveway and turned off the engine. Her first day of the job search had proved fruitless. What did, *"You're overqualified,"* mean, anyway? If she heard that phrase one more time, she'd scream. How could she be overqualified for work she knew how to do? What they meant was, they were afraid she'd keep looking for a better paying or more prestigious job and leave them in the lurch.

She got out of the vehicle and shoved the car door closed with a whoomph. There was no way she'd apply for something with a salary too low to pay her bills each month. And she wouldn't leave a new job right away as long as she could live on what she earned. Besides, there was always the chance she could move up within the company.

As she entered the house, she threw her keys and purse on the hall table, and let her briefcase fall to the floor. She hung her shawl on the coat tree, entered the living room, and plopped into the armchair. She'd better file for unemployment. They'd have resources to help her find work. Maybe she could do that online.

The people working in government agencies came to mind. When she first came to America, married Jake, and looked for a job, the government employees struck her as rude. But that was ten years ago, and she'd heard things had changed since. Government employees had lightened up, as one girl at the North Houston Regional Hospital put it. She could only hope. Her depression was bad enough without angry words assailing her ears.

She went to her desk and opened the lap drawer, took out a legal pad and pen, and began a list. What were those tips she read recently? When looking for a new job, find the best job listings. And where would she find them? Online. "Okay, number one."

Several minutes later, she went over her list. *Keep your job search focused. Build your professional brand.* What did that even mean? She scratched that line off. *Connect with your contacts. Contacts?* A deep groan escaped her lips. She'd been so distant from everyone since Jake died. It was hard to see the pity in their eyes. Easier to avoid them. She scratched that line off too.

Use job search apps and tools. Her brows pinched. That meant the computer again. As secretary to the head nurse at her old job, she knew exactly where to go online for things the nurses needed. But for her personal needs, she'd avoided the computer as much as possible. Not an option anymore.

Create a list of companies where you'd like to work. Now that one she'd do. She loved working in a clinical setting. Though not a nurse or doctor, she contributed in the effort to help people get or stay well. And clinic settings were everywhere in town.

Take the time to target your resume and cover letter. Target them? She didn't understand that when she first read it either. Okay. She'd find sites that explained how to make her resume stand out. Maybe that's what they meant. She also had to come up with a cover letter, if needed. Another item to check for online, she supposed.

Prepare to ace the interview. Right! Maybe this wasn't such a good idea. Her spirit and desire shriveled. All she could think of at the moment was making a big cup of hot chocolate, cutting a huge slice of chocolate cake, and dousing both with the entire can of whipped cream she had in the refrigerator from—when had she bought that? Probably too old.

What she needed was a pet to keep her company. People with pets always seemed happy. An animal would give her something to take care of, to talk to. She could handle that, couldn't she?

But first, chocolate.

Chapter Two

*A*lanna drummed her fingers on the kitchen counter. Two weeks had gone, and she hadn't received so much as one real job interview outside of the one with HR that first day. She measured coffee grounds into the basket and turned on the brewer. *Drat.* What a mess she'd made. She cleaned up the grounds she'd dropped onto the counter and brought her favorite mug down from the cabinet.

Dozens of pink hearts printed on the white ceramic brought to mind the Valentine morning Jake had given it to her. Her heart ached.

As she poured coffee into the cup, her cell rang. She ran to her purse in hopes the call was about a job. Her shoulders fell. Would Steve never quit? She stuffed the phone back into her purse and returned to the kitchen.

Alanna took a carton of eggs from the refrigerator, placed them on the counter next to the stove, and narrowed her eyes at them. "Why can't that man leave me alone?" She lifted an egg and held it in front of her, then tilted her head. "Not that he's not good-looking, but he's going to drive me nuts."

She tossed her head back and stared at the ceiling. She was talking to eggs. "Listen to yourself."

A plate of scrambled eggs and dry toast later, Alanna wrapped herself in her coat and headed out the door for another day of job searching. Would she be successful today? She had the experience and a glowing reference from her former boss, but neither had done her much good so far. So many people were out of work.

She slid into the driver's seat and started the engine, then gazed at herself in the rearview mirror. "Stop being a pessimist. Think positive."

Here goes nothing. She pulled into the street, bound for one of the downtown hospitals. After today, she'd have an application in every hospital in town, except for North Houston Regional.

The cell rang a second time. With high hopes for her first real interview, she connected the call without checking the display. "Hello."

"Good morning, Alanna."

Oh, fiddlesticks. "Hi, Steve. I can't talk now. I'm driving." He's persistent.

"Please don't hang up. All I want to do is help you find a new position. Look. I know a lot of people in Houston. I'm sure I can steer you in the right direction with your job search. Can we meet for coffee? I'm off today."

She shouldn't do this. It would encourage him to keep contacting her. But he *had* worked at more than one hospital in town, and he was born and raised here. Maybe he did have contacts who could help her find a good job. "If it's simply for coffee."

"Just coffee. Meet me at The Hole in the Middle Donut Shop on Highway Six near Little York Road. That's halfway between us. I can give you a list of companies that need help."

It wasn't half the distance between them, but she'd go. "Okay. I'll meet you there...when?"

"I'll leave and be there in ten minutes. I'll order for you."

Hmmm. It'd take him ten minutes compared to her driving for almost thirty. That sounded right. She'd heard he was like that, never thinking of anyone but himself. But he said he wanted to help. "Okay. I'll be there in half an hour."

Alanna pulled into the parking lot at the donut shop and spotted Steve's new red Camaro. She'd never liked red vehicles. Too flashy for her. Must be a guy thing. If he really had leads for her, this would be worth it. But he'd better keep the conversation to business and not pressure her for a date, as usual.

She opened the car door and stepped onto the pavement. He waved to her from a booth next to the front window at the far end of the shop. She waved back.

He was rather handsome, with his sandy blond hair and neatly-trimmed mustache, but not her type at all. Steve stood as she approached his table. Tall too. Yet, something about him turned her off. His mannerisms? The way he talked? His pushiness? One thing for certain, he was no Jake McCarthy. *Humph.* No man was.

Steve held his hand out for her to slide in beside him. A steaming second cup of coffee waited on the side of the table where he'd been sitting. Alanna ignored the invitation and lowered herself to the seat across the table from him.

As he reseated himself, Steve gave her the usual once-over. "Wow! You look fantastic. But you always do."

His eyes weren't on her face, never were. It was one of the things that annoyed her the most when they'd run into one another at work. Why did some men do that? He needed to refocus eighteen inches higher. "Thanks, Steve." Warmth flushed her neck.

He slid the second cup across the table to her as the right side of his lips curled upward into a smirk.

"You said you wanted to help me find a job." She wrapped her hands around the cup. "What did you have in mind?"

With a crooked smile on his face, he finally raised his eyes to hers. He moved his hand to his breast pocket, fished in it with his fingers, and furrowed his brows.

"Oh, sh...aw!" He clamped his mouth shut. "I forgot the paper at home." The half-smile returned. "I had a list of companies written out for you, names of people I'm friends with at each place." He snapped his fingers. "Hey, I've got an idea. Why don't you follow me home after we finish our coffee, and I'll give it to you? We can relax there for a while, and I'll tell you who I know works at each company."

As if she'd been watching a thriller at the movies, the hair on the back of her neck lifted. *His apartment?* Last July Fourth, he'd invited her to a party he held there. The same uncomfortable sensation hit her on that occasion. When she'd asked around at work, no one else had heard of a party at his place. "I appreciate the thought, Steve, but I don't have time to go to your apartment."

The smirk left his lips but formed again. "Okay. Let me take you to dinner tonight instead. You have to eat. I'll give you the list, and we can talk."

"I've already made plans for tonight. Sorry. Can't you email the list to me?" When his mouth drooped, and he didn't respond, she took a note pad from her bag and scribbled down her email address. As she handed it to him, he pursed his lips.

"Ri–i–ight. Okay. I can do that. Have any leads on your own yet?"

They talked for a few minutes, and she told him where she'd left her resume and filled out applications. Alanna's nerves tightened as he repeated negative comments he'd supposedly heard from employees who worked at each place.

"Please, Steve. One of these hospitals may hire me, and I don't want to go in with a negative attitude. All organizations, including medical facilities, have their downsides."

"So, you're pretty confident one of them will hire you?"

She had no intention of telling him how disappointed she'd become over her job search for the last couple of weeks. "Sorry, Steve, but I have to go." She slid out of the booth. "This afternoon, I have interviews." A lie, but a necessary one where he was concerned. "And it's getting late."

"I understand. I want to keep up with how things are going for you. I'll call you tonight."

Oh no, you don't. "Umm, tonight I have company dropping by, so I won't have time to talk. Thank you for the coffee." She turned to leave. Another little lie wouldn't hurt.

"Okay. Another time."

Not if she could help it. She rushed out the door and hurried to her car.

At the one hospital in town where she hadn't filled out an application, Alanna stepped through the front doors and located the job board outside the Human Resources Department. *Drat.* Positions for nurses and techs. Nothing else. A hard lump lodged in her chest.

During her marriage to Jake, she'd been living in a dream world. She should have prepared for the possibility of someday losing her job and continued her education. She could have been a nurse. Then she'd have lots of jobs to choose from. But Jake had never pushed her to go back to school. Nor get a job. It had been her idea to work since they decided to wait on having children. He said he'd take care of all their needs, and she could take care of him. But she needed to keep busy.

Alanna sighed. In the lower corner of the board, a small posting caught her eye. *Office Secretary.* Perfect, but why was it there instead of with the other listings? Didn't matter. She found it and could apply for the job with confidence though a hundred other secretaries tried for the same position. Maybe they hadn't posted the rest of the clerical positions yet. There was hope. She'd stop by tomorrow and check for more.

After she'd filled out the application and dropped off her resume and reference letter, she headed back to her car. Tomorrow, she'd also expand her search. Start applying at doctors' offices. That secretarial position had been the first positive sign she'd had, even if she didn't get to talk to anyone about her experience.

As Alanna unlocked the front door and walked into the living room, her phone chimed. She reached into her purse and pulled out the cell. Meghan calling from Ireland. Alanna pressed the button to connect. "Hi, big sister. What are you doing up so late? Isn't it eleven o'clock there?"

"'Ello, yourself, Ally."

Meg apologized for calling before she thought Alanna got home from work, but it was late, and she was getting sleepy. "'Aven't 'eard frum ya for too lahng, ya wee bairn."

Alanna listened to the lyrical sound of her sister's voice. Strange that her own brogue had dropped after being in the United States for ten years. Her sister teased her that she had an American accent.

Ah, dear Meg. Always talking to her as if she were her mom instead of an older sister. *"Wee bairn,"* indeed. But Meg was six years her senior. Guess living in the family home since their parents had moved to the retirement village made her feel like the matriarch of the family.

Memories of their childhood days flooded her mind as her sister gave a rundown of the nieces' and nephew's latest antics. As youngsters themselves, Meg had been in charge, no matter what they did. Like now, with their one-sided conversation.

But the thick Irish brogue was like a melody to Alanna's ears as her sister rattled on. Should she tell her she wasn't at work? Had lost her job?

"I know, Meg. Life's been a bit hectic here lately, too. But it's okay for you to call me anytime."

"I wanted to check on ya. Ya doin' okay? Ya 'ave not been yoor own self for the last few months."

How did she want to answer that? She envied Meg. Living her dream. A loving husband, three great kids, and working at home on her paintings, which were in high demand. "I'm okay."

When she got involved with Jake a little over eleven years ago, she'd been chastised by her parents and sister. It had been at her eighteenth birthday party she and Jake met. How could she blame the family for worrying when he proposed four months later? Alanna pressed her lips together. It wasn't until her and Jake's last month in Ireland that everyone felt comfortable with the idea of *this American* taking their *wee* Alanna away. The family had spent every day with him that month. She nodded at the memory. It was a miracle that Ma and Da let her marry him.

"Ally, It doesn't soond like yoo're doin' okay, yet. We're wahrried aboot you. Ya 'aven't been the same since Jake passed."

Why would she be the same, even if her family were here instead of Ireland? She'd still have the pain in her heart that had taken up residence since last December. "Meg, it's going to take time. I'm working through it. I have a couple of friends here who have me over once a week to spend time with them, plus the church family."

Although the church members hadn't been much help. She and Jake had found that church a few weeks before he died. Now the congregation avoided her. Strange that church people wouldn't understand how to act when a person lost a loved one. Maybe she was too sensitive. Could be...she was the one who avoided them. "And I have God to turn to."

The sudden silence on the other end of the line was deafening. Meg didn't like to talk about God. She'd never understood faith. Jake had tried to talk to them. But Meg and her husband always put a stop to the discussion.

"Meg, truly, I am okay. Getting better every day." *Liar*. She didn't understand God any better than Meg. Where was He in all this?

Chapter Three

*O*ver a month since she'd been laid off and no nibbles on a new job. "What am I doing wrong?" Alanna shut the laptop with a thud. With October as cold as it had been so far, the heating bills would go up. She'd have to budget more carefully.

Whatever happened to that list of companies and contacts Steve had promised to email? Not that she ever expected it to materialize. It was all a ruse to get her to go out with him. Every time he had called, and she asked about the list, he changed the subject. His response was another invitation to dinner. She grimaced. His calls were nothing but an annoyance.

But with his emails marked spam, it should eliminate some pressure. Should she block his calls altogether? Before she'd met him at the donut shop last month, she'd agreed to coffee one time while working at the hospital. She could just as easily ignore his calls.

Alanna retrieved her briefcase and purse from the hallway table. She tucked both in the coat closet on her way to the kitchen for a cup of cocoa.

She should start dinner. But what? Having postponed shopping last week to cut back on expenses left limited choices.

How much longer would unemployment pay the bills, even if she followed a strict budget? She slumped into a kitchen chair and cradled her head in her hands. Not finding a job in all this time was the pits. A tear fell onto the table.

"And where are her two so-called friends?" Invitations from Elle and Carla to hang out had dwindled down to one each since her call from Meg. It wasn't like those two to ignore her. Not on purpose. The busy season had to be the answer. With Christmas coming, everyone had tons to do. They simply hadn't realized they'd forgotten her.

Alanna pressed her hands on the table and pushed herself up, willing her body to keep moving forward. She made her way to the freezer and opened the door. The meatloaf she'd made Friday, cut up in slices and frozen for her next few dinners, stared at her. Four days of the same meal. Jake had raved about her meatloaf. She liked it too, but somehow it didn't quite perk her appetite anymore. She'd have to think of something else.

She closed the freezer door and leaned back against it. A bowl of cereal. That's what she needed. Mom's go-to when she couldn't find anything else she liked. She launched herself off the freezer door and opened the cabinet.

With a bowl of corn flakes in one hand and a cup of cocoa in the other, Alanna strolled to the couch. She set the bowl and cup on the coffee table, eased herself onto the cushions, and folded her legs under her. After wiggling herself into a comfortable position, she spooned cereal into her mouth. Milk dripped onto her chin and ran down to her blouse. "Drat! Forgot the paper towel."

Placing the bowl back on the table, she sprinted to the kitchen, tore off a section of paper towel, and wiped her mouth. She should have changed clothes first. The milk had made a mess of her favorite purple blouse. Oh well. She'd have to wash it before she wore it for an interview anyway. Wishful thinking.

As Alanna hurried back to the living room, she grabbed the remote from the top of the television and clicked it on. She repositioned herself on the couch and resumed her dinner. The television came to life with a news report. A minute into the program, the station switched to a commercial.

More Christmas ads. There were more ads on television than program time. She shrugged and clicked the TV off.

Christmas. What would she do for presents this year for her two nieces and nephew? After Jake died, her ma and da had forbidden her to send any gifts to them, adults or children, from America. They said everyone had everything they needed, and it was too much of an expense to ship from the States. Meg and Sean had jumped on that bandwagon but eventually said Alanna could send gifts to her nieces and nephew. But only if the presents were small. They'd make a dent in her budget this year.

Perhaps she should look online for something for the kids. But what would interest them? She hadn't a clue. They'd grown up so fast. *Gift cards?*

Christmas. She didn't want to think about Christmas. Another one without Jake. It was easy to understand why some people were so depressed at this time of year. Those who'd never gone through a loss around the holidays didn't understand. The world would continue to spin, regardless of who had a broken heart.

A vision of the old family home in Ireland, decorated for the holidays, flooded her mind. Her family would pay her way to come home. But they'd want her to stay once they found out she had no job. She loved living in America. Homesickness tugged at her heart. She and Jake had bought this house...together. And she was a U.S. citizen.

She loved Ireland too, but this was the home she wanted. "Jake's here," she whispered. "Not in Ireland." At least his body was. And so many memories. Heaven was his real home now. He'd always reminded her it would be. And how it would be hers too, someday. Would it be? She'd never had that assurance. But she had to believe he was there.

"Better not get too deep in thoughts like that." The devil would give her another push on the slide to deeper depression. "No. You'll not have me goin' there, devil." Alanna stomped both feet to the floor, tromped to the kitchen, and dropped off her empty bowl and cup in the sink.

Grabbing her jacket and an afghan, she slipped out the front door. Time for some fresh air. Regardless of the cold.

Alanna trudged across the porch to the swing, wrapped the afghan around her, and closed her eyes. The quiet evening on the cul-de-sac served as a calming salve to her nerves. Her feet moved the swing back and forth rhythmically. After dinner, it had been her and Jake's favorite place to talk over the events of the day. He'd bought the swing for her last birthday. Such a good man. So loving.

She opened her eyes and gazed out over the neighbors' yards. Christmas lights would soon illuminate each of the other seven houses on their street. Each year, she and Jake had watched the families decorate on Thanksgiving weekend. Then Jake would tell her how he'd like to decorate their house. He'd listen to her ideas too, and they'd complete their plans before the end of the next week. Maybe she should decorate this year. It might make her feel better. Maybe.

Tears welled in her eyes. She swiped them away with a corner of the afghan. *Should I go home to Ireland?*

Chapter Four

epressed from another day of submitting applications at every office she could find seeking clerical help, Alanna changed into her sweats. It was Friday. She could relax for the weekend, now.

She donned her winter jacket, grabbed the afghan from the couch, and retreated to the front porch, hoping some peaceful time outside would erase the trademark mantra she kept hearing from businesses, "You're overqualified for this job."

As she swayed on the swing, Alanna blew a frustrated puff of air and closed her eyes. She leaned back and rested her head on the side chain, listening to the familiar squeak. A sense of not being alone overwhelmed her. "Jake. You said you'd always be with me."

Was God with her? She had such good memories to comfort her in times of loneliness. Had God brought her and Jake together, sending him to Ireland on business when someone else should have been there instead? How often she'd heard stories of how God placed the right people in the right places, according to His will. But where had He been when she really needed Him? When Jake was dying. Why had He let her beloved husband die?

As something touched her leg, Alanna's eyes popped open, and she caught her breath. She glanced down and exhaled. "Hello."

A long-haired orange tabby rubbed against her. Two feet behind the cat sat a short-haired dog, its cream-colored coat peppered with light brown freckles. The dog wagged its tail slowly, as if unsure of its welcome.

"Where did you two come from? I've never seen you in the neighborhood before. Are we neighbors?"

It was all the dog needed. It approached Alanna with its tongue lolling out on one side. Its tail gaily swept back and forth.

"I see from the plumbing...and excuse me if that's rude...you are a female," she told the dog. The cat jumped up onto the swing beside Alanna. "Looks like your feline friend is too."

The dog laid her head on Alanna's knee and peered at her with sad golden eyes, while the cat curled up next to Alanna's leg.

"You each wear a matching collar, so I guess you escaped from your house somehow." Alanna checked for tags. "Hmmm. The only identification on either of you is your name."

She laid her hand on the dog's head. "So, you're Susie, huh?" Susie wagged her tail and opened her mouth as if she were smiling, ears at attention. Alanna scratched her behind the ears with both hands and then turned her attention to the cat. "And you, little fuzz face, are Marmalade." She stroked the cat's thick, orange fur. "Very appropriate. And your green eyes are gorgeous."

The vibration from the cat's strong purr reminded Alanna of a hand massager. "I sure hope you two can find your way home. Looks like you've been well cared for. Bet you don't live too far away."

The dog curled up at Alanna's feet and stayed there until she rose to go inside. "Thanks for visiting me, Susie...Marmalade. You'd better be off to your own homes. I need to go in." She stroked each of them one more time and went inside.

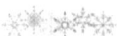

Early the following morning, Alanna awoke to a cold bedroom. She hadn't listened to the weather report, but it must have been colder than normal last night.

She dressed in a pink sweater, her favorite scrubby jeans, and thick, fuzzy pink socks. As she headed for the living room, she checked the temperature on the thermostat in the hall. "Sixty-five degrees? No wonder I'm cold." Back in Ireland, she would have considered this a heatwave. At this time of year, her family would be dealing with forty-something degrees. But she had acclimated to the warm southern temperature of Texas after a couple of years. She flipped the lever to heat and adjusted the arrow to a lower temperature than she'd been used to. That should keep the gas bill from skyrocketing. She'd survive.

Alanna finished her trek down the hallway and peeked out the front door window. No newspaper in sight. The delivery boy had once told her he liked to see if he could land it in the swing. She opened the door and looked toward the end of the porch.

Susie and Marmalade lay scrunched up into a ball in the corner next to the house. The dog shivered.

Alanna hurried to the animals. "Oh no! You poor dears...out in this weather all night. You must be used to a warm house. I'll bet you're lost and scared."

Tears sprung to Alanna's eyes. How could she have been so thoughtless? When she left them sitting on the porch, she'd assumed they'd find their way home. "Oh, God. I feel terrible. Please let them be okay."

Susie lifted her head with her ears flattened and licked Marmalade's head.

"Best friends, huh." Alanna squatted and patted Susie. "Best friends are important." She stroked Marmalade.

The cat opened one eye, and a hoarse mew came out.

"Come into the house. You need to get warm and eat. I'm sure I can find something for you."

Susie struggled to rise as if her joints were stiff. Alanna rubbed her back while Marmalade brushed past the dog's hind legs.

A minute later, the animals followed Alanna through the living room, down the hallway, and into the kitchen. She turned on the oven to add warmth to the room. From the top cabinet, she brought down a large bowl, filled it with water, and placed it on the floor.

The dog and cat rushed to the bowl and lapped water as if they hadn't had a drop for days. Alanna shook her head. "Oh, dear." The tears she'd held back slid down her cheeks.

She rummaged through the cabinets but found nothing suitable to feed a cat and dog. From the freezer, she pulled a plastic bag containing two cooked chicken breasts from her dinner the week before. Good thing she hadn't found them anymore appetizing than the meatloaf last night. She also took out a container of leftover rice from the refrigerator. "I've heard that rice and chicken are good for dogs. I hope the same is true for cats, Marmalade."

After she'd defrosted the chicken in the microwave, Alanna cut the meat into tiny chunks and mixed it with the leftover rice. She refilled the dry water bowl, but the pets had drunk their fill. They sat on their haunches and watched while Alanna got two more bowls from the cabinet.

She spooned a small amount of food into each. "Don't want to give you too much right away. If you were that thirsty, there's no telling when you've eaten last. We'll start with this." The animals rushed to gulp down the chicken and rice as soon as the bowls hit the floor.

They inhaled the food, poor little dears. She'd better wait a while before giving them more.

The animals sat next to the bowls as Alanna made a second search through the cabinets for food she might feed them. She'd have to run to the store and buy some dog and cat food. She certainly wasn't going to turn these poor creatures out to fend for themselves.

Alanna found two cans of tuna in the back of the shelf. "Aha. I know you can eat this. And I'll cook more rice. It should hold you until I go to the store." She turned to face them. "But what will I do with you when I go out?" The pets followed her to the table.

When she took a seat, Susie laid her head on Alanna's and peered up with her sad eyes. Marmalade purred and rubbed against Alanna's jeans. She patted both of them on the head. "I guess you'll be okay in the house alone. Don't worry, I'll take care of you until I find out who you belong to. And if I don't find your owners, I was considering a pet for myself anyway. I'll have two instead of one."

She would love having these two adorable furballs for company. For the first time in days, Alanna smiled.

God, is this Your doing?

Chapter Five

*M*onday morning, Alanna loaded a hammer, nails, and a stack of computer-generated flyers into the backseat of her car. The pictures of Susie and Marmalade had come out perfectly. The two animal shelters she'd contacted said they had no dog or cat that looked like the pair on record, but they'd be happy to upload the picture on their site. She hopped into the driver's seat.

By the time she finished posting the flyers in her neighborhood and the next subdivision, she had traveled a few miles from home. Now to the supermarket for pet food. She'd ask the manager to post a flyer in the window or on the bulletin board.

As she turned onto the last street before the store, a flyer on a post at the stop sign caught her eye. Was that Susie and Marmalade? *Sure looks like them.*

Alanna parked the car, hopped out, and rushed to the post. She stared at the weather-faded paper. It had to be the same cat and dog, being hugged by a man. A very handsome man, despite the worn picture. How long had this paper hung there? How long had the poor dears been lost? *Oh, no.* The owner's information at the bottom was torn off.

From behind her came the sound of a throat being cleared. She jumped. When she spun, the handsome face from the poster gazed at her. She gulped.

The man smiled, revealing a dimple in his right cheek, and took a step back. "Sorry if I startled you. I was in a hurry. Almost ran right into you. I came to take that paper down."

Alanna's mouth opened. No words came out. He had the shiniest, silvery-gray eyes.

"Ah, I hate to be rude, miss, but you're standing in my way, and I need to return to work. Why were you staring at the picture? Have you seen my dog and cat?" As he grimaced, he rubbed his jaw. "Those aren't your pets, are they?"

She needed to get herself together. It wasn't as if she'd never seen a good-looking man before. "Well, actually. Yes. No. Actually." *You sound intelligent.* "I'm sorry. I guess you did startle me. Are they your pets?"

"Well, actually, yes. I mean, no." He burst into a hearty laugh. "What I mean is, I've taken care of them for some time. Last spring, they showed up at my apartment complex in terrible shape, as if they'd been running through brambles. Pretty pathetic. I took them in, cleaned them, and then placed those flyers around the complex and the rest of the neighborhood hoping to find their owner. The two of them were obviously buddies."

"But, you didn't get any calls?"

"Not one. I forgot about the posters until today."

Alanna nodded. "So, how did you lose them?"

"A month ago, my housekeeper failed to close the door all the way when she took out the trash. When she came back, the door stood wide open. The animals were gone. She felt terrible and searched everywhere in the apartment complex."

He smiled again, and Alanna's pulse increased.

"She'd become fond of the sweet little girls." His brows rose. "So, are they yours?"

"Not really. The dog and cat showed up at my house Friday night." A prick of guilt sliced through Alanna. She shouldn't have left them out in the cold. "They were still there Saturday morning...and hungry. I thought they lived in the neighborhood and would find their way back home."

As her eyes flooded, she closed them. "The poor dears were huddled in the corner of my porch, shivering." She opened her eyes. "I wasn't sure if it was because they were cold or scared. I should have taken them into the house when I went inside, but I did the next morning...and fed them. Then I made flyers to post in the neighborhood on my way to the store to buy food for them."

His third smile set butterflies loose in her stomach.

His brows rose. "They're okay, right?

"Yes, no thanks to me."

"But it is thanks to you, miss. If you hadn't taken them in and fed them, they'd be wandering the streets and hungry. Could have gotten run over. But Susie and Marmalade are safe."

"If you think of it that way, yes." Alanna gazed into his eyes.

"If your flyers are in a different neighborhood, someone might see them this time." He removed the tattered paper from the pole. "They're such beautiful, friendly animals. They must have had a good home. But their family may have been among those affected by the Memorial Day flooding last year. The pets could have been lost, and the family moved away."

"That's what I thought. The animals sure are sweet."

"When they went missing from my apartment, I called the rescue shelters and filled out paperwork. Posted online and got zilch." The man pulled his lips to the side.

"Same here." Alanna's heart slumped as she once more dropped her gaze to the ground. "I suppose you want them back."

The man tilted his head. "What a sad expression. I see they won you over as fast as they did me." He held out his hand to her. "I'm Chris. Christopher Maguire."

She placed her hand in his, and a tingle ran up her arm. "Alanna McCarthy. And they did latch onto my heart, even before I felt so guilty, leaving them out in the cold through the night. Would you like to pick them up?" A twinge darted through her at the thought of Susie's sad eyes. Had he mistreated them? Was that why the dog was so sad? Why they ran away?

He didn't seem to be that kind of a man. And why would he bother posting flyers to find them if he didn't love them?

When she pulled her hand away, he looked at his for a moment and dropped it to his side. "I don't want to break your heart by taking them away. Tell you what. Why don't I go home with you to see them, and we'll let them decide who they want to live with." He raised his brows. "If you don't mind, that is."

A strange man following her home? Meg would kill her if she knew. She stared into his soft gray eyes, back at the flyer with his image on it, and then gazed toward the street where a new silver Malibu had parked behind her car. She glanced back at him. The sadness in his eyes matched Susie's. He must miss them. "Okay. I guess it's all right."

"I understand your apprehension. The only thing you know about me so far is my name."

So far?

He dug into his back pocket and drew out a wallet, opened it, and held out an identification card.

Christopher Maguire, MD. Where had she seen that name before? *Right.* On the front of the clinic next door to Fairbrook Hospital where she'd put in an application last week. One of their doctors.

His gray eyes surrounded by jet black eyelashes matching his wavy hair sent goosebumps up her arms. What a heartthrob. The dimple in his right cheek showed, and she melted inside like hot butter. Female patients, no doubt, swooned at the sight of him. "Thank you. You can follow me." *Anywhere.*

Cut it out, Alanna. You're asking for trouble.

Chris parked his Malibu at the curb as Alanna pulled her car into the driveway. After slipping out of the driver's seat, she leaned against the door and waited for him. What a beautiful woman.

As he reached her, he glanced at her home. "Charming house. I'm sure the critters are more comfortable in this nice ranch than closed up in my small apartment while I'm at work. And you have a fenced-in yard too."

She smiled and lifted a set of keys from the side pocket of her purse.

Why had he gotten attached to those two four-legged ragamuffins anyway? He'd never had pets before. His heart sagged. "Something tells me they won't be jumping into my lap to go home with me." He tried to laugh, but it came out more of a grunt.

Alanna's brows furrowed as she unlocked the door. She stepped into the foyer and held the door for Chris to enter. When she turned, she called, "Here Susie...here kitty, kitty, kitty."

The dog and cat came running from the back of the house and skidded to a halt halfway through the living room. They sat on their haunches at the same time, as if joined at the hip. And in unison, tilted their heads one way, looking at him, then the other, looking at Alanna. Their tails remained motionless, as though the animals were trying to figure out how these two humans wound up in the same house.

As Susie and Marmalade continued their pendulum routine, Chris lowered himself to one knee and held out his arms. "Susie? Marmalade? Come here." He patted the thigh of his bent leg.

They stared at him for a second and then Alanna.

She took a few steps away from Chris and knelt on the floor, extending one hand. "Come, girls."

They stood. But didn't move.

Chris and Alanna rose and faced one another. He shrugged. "They can't make up their minds? Or what?"

The cat and dog ran to Chris and jumped up onto his leg. A second later, they ran to Alanna. Back and forth they ran between them as if they were happy to see them together. Susie's tail wagged, and Marmalade's purr sounded like a motor.

Alanna laughed. Chris chuckled.

They knelt again and pet each furball until Chris stood and helped Alanna to her feet. "Joint custody?"

"Really?"

Her face revealed a collage of questions, surprise, and joy. He'd seen enough in the medical field to gauge a woman's emotions. "Why not? They've fallen as much in love with you...as I—we—have with them." *Be careful of those first emotional impressions, Maguire.* He knew nothing about this woman, lovely though she was. He'd just met her. How could he—this fast? He'd been with her less than an hour. Did that happen in the real world? Love at first sight?

"I've got an idea. Why don't we run over to my place and pick up a supply of the food I have for them, one of the beds I've acquired, and whatever toys you think they might like while they're with you...instead of your buying anything. They've been gone from my place a whole month now, and it would be good to use up the big bags of food I opened right before they got out. I've kept the food sealed, so it's good."

She shouldn't have agreed to go to his apartment. But she hadn't wanted to act weird. Alanna glanced in the rearview mirror at Chris in his Malibu, following her from his home.

But he'd been a perfect gentleman. Kept his apartment door open the entire time they were there and while he phoned his office to explain why he'd be late.

Alanna snickered. He sure had gone all out for the two furbabies. Three beds, each large enough for them to sleep comfortably. One for the front room, one in the office, and she'd assumed the third for the bedroom from what he said. Pet bowls of every color. And the toys. Wow. They had their own toy box. Chris would make a wonderful dad someday. A twinge of pain shot through her. Jake would have too.

She took another look in the rearview mirror and shoved her sorrow to the back of her mind.

A few minutes later, they entered the foyer to a warm welcome from the dog and cat.

Chris deposited the box full of pet supplies in the kitchen. He filled each pet's bowl with food and placed it in the corner of the room. "Is this area okay?"

Alanna searched the room. "Seems the best place to me. Thanks. I can't believe the collection of toys you had for them."

"First-time pet owner. I guess I went a little crazy at the pet store." He chuckled. "It was fun though. And I'm glad I got them since you need a collection here too."

She stifled a laugh. "Thank you. I appreciate not having to buy anything since I lost—" Alanna spun to the counter and closed the two bags of pet food. "I'm on a budget, to keep the bills low."

Steps sounded behind her, and he leaned an elbow on the counter next to her, a large pet bed hanging from his fingertips. "Aha. A frugal woman. It's to be commended." He pushed himself upright with his elbow and strode into the living room with the pet bed. "Where should I put this?"

"Next to the couch. I spend a lot of time reading there. It'll be nice to have the company." She joined Chris and found him staring at Susie and Marmalade, who were curled up on one end of the sofa together. Each snored softly.

He shook his head and snickered. "They did the same thing at my place. I should have warned you."

She placed her hand over her mouth and giggled. "Sin ceart go leor."

Chris's head spun. His mouth dropped open. "What did you say?"

"Oops. I'm sorry. I said that's okay. When I was a lass, our pets slept on the couch. You're no eejit." Her Irish brogue slipped out.

"Eejit? And what was the language you spoke in?"

"Sorry again. I revert to Gaelic on occasion. Especially if I'm tired. And eejit is our slang for idiot, which you're not." She laughed.

"You speak Irish?"

"It's what my parents speak most of the time. I've forgotten much of it, although I understand it fluently."

Chris shook his head. "My grandparents spoke Gaelic, but I never picked it up. You're a very interesting woman, Alanna McCarthy."

His cell phone buzzed, and he drew it from his pocket. "Hello?"..."Yes."..."Okay, I'll be a few minutes more. Apologize to Mr. Drew for me, and tell him I'm on my way."

He ended the call and gave her a cockeyed smile. "I'm sorry, I'll have to run out on you."

Run out on her? As if they were old friends and had a whole afternoon planned? Although, she sure wished they had. She followed him to the door.

"I have a patient waiting for me." He turned to her and took a deep breath. "Alanna, you'll be the other half of this parenting team for those two." He nodded at the pets sleeping soundly on the couch.

Her gaze followed his.

"I think that means we should get to know one another better." He grinned. "Would you allow me to take you to dinner tonight? Steaks, or whatever you like."

She studied his face. Was he serious? Did he think they needed to nail down the joint custody rules and parenting style? *What should I do?*

"I'd love to." *Alanna! What are you thinking?*

"Good." He gave her one of his office cards. "Call my office in an hour and ask for me. I'll tell the receptionist to expect your call. That way, we can decide where to have dinner."

She stared at the card. Steaks on her budget were impossible. She glanced up at his eyes. Whatever his motivation, she could enjoy a tasty steak. He was so handsome. And it was too late to back out.

Chapter Six

*A*lanna peered through the peephole. Chris stared at the door as if he could see her through the tiny glass. He must know what that smile of his did to her insides after...what, their sixth date since meeting a month ago. She swung the door open.

He stepped into the foyer and held pink carnations out to her. "Hope your day went as well as mine."

Tingles ran up her arms as she gaped at the bouquet. The first time she'd received any since Jake died. She closed her mouth, and her eyes misted. He'd often brought them home for her, knowing they were her favorite flower.

"Have I done something wrong, Alanna?"

"No. Thank you. How did you guess I love carnations?"

"For a second, I thought you were going to cry. Was it okay for me to give you flowers?"

"Of course. It was very thoughtful of you."

He grinned. "Today is our one-month anniversary, and you struck me as a pink carnation kind of girl."

"Girl?" Her brows rose. A man who knew how long he'd been seeing a woman. Would miracles never end? She stifled a laugh. If he kept saying sweet things like that to her, she'd be hopelessly in love with him before long. "It's been a while since anyone gave me flowers."

"And it stirred a memory."

"How do you know these things?"

"We doctors are trained to notice responses. Part of the job description."

Another smile. Had he also noticed what it did to her?

"Are you ready to leave for dinner, or should I practice patience?" He spun toward the living room. "And where are our four-legged kids?"

"Susie had to go out, and of course, Marmalade had to accompany her. I've never seen a dog and cat so attached to one another."

"They remind me of those pre-teen girls who need to go everywhere together, even the restroom." He chuckled. "It's special to cherish someone so much you can't be apart." He winced.

Now *he'd* experienced a memory. It hurt to know something upset him. Maybe she was already in love. "Let me get the *kids* in, and we can leave." She hurried to the kitchen. "I'm hungry."

Chris followed.

Alanna glanced back at him. "When you suggested Bob's Steak House tonight, my mouth watered." She opened the back door, and the dog and cat bounded in. "Bob's is a favorite of mine."

Susie jumped up on Chris's right leg, and Marmalade rubbed against the left.

"Hey, guys. You'll get hair on my pants." He laughed and bent to pet each, winking at Alanna. "Hope you don't mind if I wear fur leggings tonight."

She chortled and raised a finger. "Be right back." She left them in the kitchen and rushed to her bedroom. When she returned, she handed him a lint roller. "This should take care of the fur."

They left the kitchen, and Chris sat on the arm of the living room chair, moving the lint roller across the legs of his dark gray slacks. Alanna sat on the edge of the couch. He was so handsome. The robin's egg blue shirt under a gray sports coat set off his magnificent silvery eyes.

He handed the hair-covered roller back to her. "You look beautiful in that dress."

She blushed. Little did he know she'd spent thirty minutes trying on outfits before she chose the violet one.

"It brings out the green in your eyes."

What a charmer. Her insides quivered. *Is he for real?* She'd have to pinch herself to make sure this wasn't a dream.

He stood and reached for her hand. "We'd better go before my stomach revolts. There was no time for lunch today. Only had crackers midafternoon."

"Oh. I could've made dinner here tonight if you were that hungry." Although, she didn't have much in the way of man-type food in the house. Not much of any food, since she'd stuck to such a strict budget until she could find a new job.

"That's okay. I was messing with you. It's not the first time I've skipped lunch because of walk-in patients." He led her to the front door, and they glanced back to the living room.

Susie jumped onto the couch, circled once, and eased herself into the corner. Marmalade hopped up next to her and snuggled. Both animals fixed their gaze on the couple.

Chris turned the doorknob. "It's as if those two know we're going out for steak. They're on their best behavior, anticipating a doggie bag when we return." He laughed.

Chris held the door for Alanna to enter Bob's Steak House. His eyes traveled to her curvaceous figure as she stepped ahead of him. The skirt of her dress swayed as she walked. His line of sight drifted to her shapely legs. *Wow.* He sure had stumbled onto a beaut of a girl the day they met. With a perfect personality to match.

She turned and tilted her head. "Are you coming?"

He glanced over his shoulder. No one there. "Yes. Thought someone was behind us." He pulled his mouth to one side as the corners of her lips turned upward. Smart cookie. She knew exactly what he'd been doing. He returned her grin.

Chris caught up with Alanna, and they approached the hostess.

"Table for two, sir?"

"Yes, two." Before he'd met Alanna, it'd been a long time since he'd asked a woman out. The few dates he'd had earlier this year hadn't worked out. Reminded him too much of— *No.* He would *not* spoil this evening with bad memories.

The hostess handed a waiter the menus. The young man swung his arm toward the dining area. Chris followed Alanna, noting her graceful gait.

At the table, Chris seated her and draped her white knitted shawl over the back of the chair. As he took in the aroma of grilled steak, he swallowed to avoid drooling.

The waiter placed menus in front of them. "Need a few minutes to decide?"

Without opening his, Chris said, "I'm having filet mignon." Each time he'd taken her out, she'd ordered the least expensive choice on the menu. He'd bet she was conservative in most areas. "Filet for you, too, Alanna?"

"That sounds good."

Chris nodded as the waiter turned to her.

She smiled. "Filet it is, medium rare."

"And your side dish? The macaroni and cheese is a house specialty and particularly good."

"Perfect."

"And to drink? A glass of wine?"

"No wine. I'd prefer a glass of water with a slice of lime, if I may?"

"Very well." The young man turned to Chris. "And your sides, sir?"

"The lady read my mind. The same for me, except for the water. I'd prefer iced tea."

"Good choice, sir. Will that be sweet or unsweet?"

"Unsweet."

After the waiter left with their order, Chris observed Alanna's face as she searched the room, rich interior, and chandelier. She stared at the stained-glass ceiling. A far-away smile formed on her lips.

"Pleasant thought?"

Her eyes focused on his. "I was recalling a time when...oh, you don't want to hear this."

"Yes, I do."

She dropped her eyes to her folded hands on the table.

"Unless it would bother you to tell me."

Her lashes rose, and her green eyes sparkled as if they had misted over. The smile returned.

Alanna opened her mouth. Then closed it. Her lips puckered for a moment. "To speak of this to anyone else, yes, it would hurt. But not to you. Is it weird for me to talk about my late husband?"

"Not at all. If you're comfortable with it."

During salad and the main course, Alanna told Chris about her marriage to Jake and what a wonderful husband he had been. "We came here often. Jake even suggested we install a stained-glass ceiling like this one in our dining room."

"Sounds like a great guy. I wish I had met him."

"He was." Her gaze fell. "The heart attack came so fast. It was over before anyone could do anything. A shock."

"We men tend to take our health for granted."

Her eyes widened. "You don't have a heart problem, do you?"

He reached across the table and touched her hand, resting next to the dinner plate. "No. I'm in excellent health. Being a physician in a clinic, I get regular checkups. God has been good to me, considering the recklessness of my youth."

"Weren't we all reckless?" She giggled softly.

"I suppose so. Crazy teenagers."

As they finished their dinner, the waiter reappeared at the table. "May I interest you in dessert? Coffee?" He handed dessert menus to both of them.

Chris winked at Alanna. "Order something you've always wanted to try. Let's make this a special evening."

She bit her bottom lip and smiled. "I've had my eye on that Baked Alaska. It sounds so good, but it's for two people."

With his eyes glued to hers, Chris handed his dessert menu back to the waiter. "Baked Alaska for two. And coffee." He raised his brows. "You too?"

"Yes, please." She glanced at the young man and handed him her menu. "Make mine decaf."

The waiter withdrew.

"Chris, you've spoiled me. I won't be satisfied with anything I can make at home now."

"As long as you keep smiling, it's worth it. But I'll bet you're a fantastic cook. You could have whipped up this same meal with no trouble."

She laughed and fidgeted with her napkin. "I can cook. Jake used to tell me my cooking was better than his mother's," she looked up, "but I was never to tell her he said it." She giggled. "But it's hard to cook good meals when you have to—"

Why had she stopped mid-sentence? Her lashes drooped again, and the smile was gone. "When you have to what, Alanna? Why did you interrupt yourself? What's wrong? Please, tell me."

Her eyes met his. She glanced around the room. Her forehead wrinkled. "Okay. But I don't want you to feel sorry for me. And please don't say I can't keep Susie and Marmalade part-time as we agreed. I need them since...I lost my job." Her eyes closed, and her head dropped forward.

He lifted her chin with an index finger and peered at her. "Don't worry. I won't take Susie and Marmalade from you. How long have you been out of work?"

Alanna shared how the hospital let her go. "It was a hospital-wide layoff."

"But you've filed for unemployment, right?"

She nodded. "Unemployment covers the bills if I'm careful with my budgeting. But I really need to find a job. The market for my skills is sparse."

"What did you do at the hospital?"

"Secretary to the nursing supervisor. I loved my job. Felt as if I was right there helping the patients along with the nurses. That is, until I was let go."

"Have you applied at Fairbrook Clinic, where I work?"

"Yes. For a secretarial position listed on the hospital job board right before we met. The only one available, and I was told it was for the clinic. But they'd received many applications, so I'm not surprised I didn't get it."

Chris lifted his cell out of his pocket and pressed a few numbers. "Excuse me for a moment. This is very important. Back in a second." He rose from the table and hurried to the restaurant lobby.

Chapter Seven

*A*lanna's gaze followed Chris to the restaurant entrance. What prompted that? Maybe something he forgot regarding a patient. It was rather abrupt, though. She placed her napkin on the plate, rose, and headed for the ladies' room.

She washed her hands and stared into the restroom mirror. *God, if You're there, please help me with these growing emotions I have for Chris. Or do You even care how I feel?*

As she approached the table, Chris stood. "Are you okay? Your face is flushed." He held the chair out for her.

"I'm fine."

"Sorry for dashing out of the room. It was a call I couldn't put off until later." He reseated himself.

"I figured it had to be important."

He cocked his head and smiled.

The waiter brought the Baked Alaska, placed it in the middle of the table, and ignited the dessert. After the flames extinguished, leaving a layer of toasted meringue, he set plates in front of Alanna and Chris. "Enjoy." The young man left.

"Allow me." Chris took the serving utensil and cut into the mound of browned meringue. He put a sizable slice onto her plate and then served himself. "This looks delicious. I've never had it."

"Really? I sure hope you like it."

"Your eyes told me I would." He laughed. "I try new things all the time. And strawberry is one of my favorite flavors."

Alanna lifted a forkful into her mouth. "Mmm. This is incredible. The strawberry ice cream, combined with the chocolate cake on the bottom, is a perfect combination." She laid the fork down and gazed at Chris. "Thank you for the superb meal and treat. Now I *will* have to make dinner for you."

"I'll take that as an invitation. You tell me when."

Butterflies fluttered through her insides as if shaken from a bush. A nice quiet dinner at home with Chris. She bit her lower lip.

"Alanna, you're not eating your share of the Baked Alaska."

She stared at his lips, his eyes, hair, and back to his eyes. How was it possible there could be another man so wonderful? She'd been blessed.

"Earth to Alanna."

"Sorry. Guess I'm tired. It's been a strenuous couple of months, and it's catching up with me."

"With the situation you've been handed, I can understand. Are you sure you want the responsibility of a dog and a cat? I can take them home tonight, and you can tell me when you want them back."

"Oh no, you don't. You're not getting Susie or Marmalade until your agreed-to time, Doctor Maguire." She snickered.

His gray eyes sparkled from the lamp on the table. "That's my girl."

His girl? A figure of speech. *Don't read more into it than there is.*

Yips and meows greeted Alanna and Chris upon their return from dinner. They hurried to the kitchen, the pets close on their heels. Alanna took two clean plates from the cabinet. "You'd think they'd never eaten before." As she peeked down to see where the animals were, she opened the box and dangled a chunk of steak over it. "Wait'll you taste what we brought for you."

Chris took the meat from her and cut the steak into pieces while the animals bounced. He laughed. "For sure, their noses are in perfect working order." He washed his hands while Alanna lowered the dishes to the floor.

The meat disappeared in seconds. The pets looked up at them, Susie wagging her tail and Marmalade's twitching with excitement.

"You're welcome." She shook her finger at them. "You shouldn't eat so fast. You'll get more later."

While Chris rinsed the dishes in the sink, Alanna placed the rest of the meat in the refrigerator. She turned. "Care for more coffee?"

"It's getting late." He peeked at his watch. "Almost ten o'clock. You sure you're not too tired?"

Could he be more thoughtful? "I'm fine."

"But you zoned out for a second at the restaurant. I don't want you to get sick."

She sighed. Did he want to leave?

Chris touched her shoulder. "Truth be told, I'm a night owl, so it's not too late for me."

"I am tired. But not too tired. And...I have a hunch things are picking up for me." She spun to the counter, butterflies all aflutter inside her. "I'll make coffee."

"I've got the same hunch." As he propped his elbow beside her on the counter, he faced her and grinned.

Chapter Eight

Alanna awoke the next morning with a smile. She'd dreamed of Chris throughout the night. What a beautiful way to start the day. She swung her legs out of bed and pushed the white lace window curtains open. The world greeted her with birdsong and a bright ray of sunshine through the cedar tree. Her joy was contagious. Nature felt it.

After dressing in a Navy blue suit and a white blouse, she replenished the dry food in Susie and Marmalade's dishes, gave them a fresh bowl of water, and let them out into the backyard. She helped herself to a bowl of oat cereal. Even the same old cereal tasted better today. Coffee washed down the last morsels from her bowl, and she placed the dishes into the dishwasher.

Alanna opened the back door. "Susie, Marmalade. Come in." They bounded into the kitchen, drawing a whoosh of crisp, cold air with them.

She grabbed her briefcase and purse from the coffee table and swung her multicolored knit poncho over her suit. Before opening the front door, she scratched each animal's ears and waited until they hopped onto the end of the couch, where they settled themselves into one furry ball of adorable. "So sweet."

Her cell rang. "Oh, no. Here we go. Steve." She'd not let him ruin her day by pressuring her for a date. She'd made her disinterest clear. Alanna jammed the cell to the bottom of her purse without looking at the screen. "Wait! She'd blocked him." She yanked it out. The missed call showed a number from another city. Probably a robocall. "Nuts." Wish it had been Chris.

She left the house, started the car, and slid the gear into reverse to pull out of the driveway. As her phone rang again, she moaned. But it might be a place where she'd applied for work. She dug in her purse and retrieved the cell on the fourth ring. *Not another robocall.* She threw the phone back into her bag. *They're a nuisance.*

As she drove to the first doctor's office on her list to apply for work, she glanced at her wristwatch. Too early. They wouldn't open until nine. Fifteen minutes to wait. The cell jangled. She rolled her eyes. "Oh, brother." Alanna pressed a button to connect, hoping to get a live person so she could tell them to take her off their list. "*Hello.*"

"Good morning, Alanna. I must have called too early, judging from the tone in your voice."

"Chris."

"Or did you not have a pleasant night's sleep?"

She giggled to herself. If he only knew. "Sorry, Chris. I've been getting robocalls. I *did* have a good night's sleep. Did you?"

"*Superb.*"

His voice held a lightheartedness. Had he experienced dreams similar to hers? She shook her head. *Dream on.* "And what can I do for you this morning, sir?"

The chuckle he gave made her heart leap. "Seriously, I didn't phone too early, did I? You did say you planned more job hunting today."

Every time Steve had called in the morning, it was before she'd had a chance to wash the sleep from her face. "Not too early at all."

"I know you have a busy day ahead, but I thought you might spare a moment for coffee with me at The Hot Brew Coffee Shop next to the clinic. I have something to tell you."

Had he changed his mind? He didn't want to share Susie and Marmalade? "Sure, I don't have any set appointments. Coffee sounds good."

"Outstanding. I'll meet you there."

Alanna walked through the doors of The Hot Brew and zeroed in on Chris, who waited in a far corner. Two steaming cups sat on either side of the table. He saw her and waved.

Her pounding heart all but drowned out the click of her heels on the tile floor as she approached the smiling hunk of male in a pristine lab coat. The crisp white contrasted with his thick, black hair.

When she arrived at the table, he stood and motioned for her to slide into the chair across from him.

"Thanks for the coffee, Chris. Great way to start what I hope will be a successful day of job hunting for me."

"I'm sure it will be, as a matter-of-fact." The right side of his lips curled upward as if he held a secret.

"Thanks for the confidence."

"I have a surprise. Hopefully, a pleasant one. Remember that call I made last night at the restaurant?"

"Yes." He had good news about one of his patients, no doubt. She sipped her coffee and peered at him over the cup rim. He wanted to share it with her. How sweet.

"When you told me you'd applied for the secretarial position our office had posted at the hospital, I phoned Mandy, the HR Manager for our clinic. We've been friends for ages, so I knew she wouldn't mind the after-hours call. She had filled the position, but the girl she hired didn't work out. I told Mandy I'd met you, and she said she'd dig out your application."

Alanna caught her breath. "That was kind of you."

He stretched his arms toward her and took her hands in his. "The thing is, the position is as my secretary." He winked. "Not my personal secretary, but secretary to both me and my partner."

Alanna's jaw dropped. Chris lifted her chin up with his index finger. He puckered his lips and then grinned. His gray eyes danced with amusement, and his dimple deepened.

"Your secretary?"

His brows pinched together. "Is this good or bad? Not sure how to take the reaction. You'd be the clinic secretary, working for both me and my partner, along with helping the office manager." Question marks flooded his face as he gazed at her.

"I guess I'm in shock. Why didn't you tell me when you came back to the table last night? I thought your call was about a patient."

"Mandy didn't answer her phone, and I had to leave a message. I didn't want to raise your hopes if she'd already hired someone new. She didn't get back to me until early this morning."

"I understand."

"Efficient office manager that she is, Mandy said she wanted to check references before she approved your application. When I arrived at the clinic this morning, I went straight to her office. She'd beat me in. Said she had a feeling this was important to me and to go ahead with an interview while she completed the reference checks. So, here we are." He leaned forward. "Interviewing." He raised his brows.

Alanna's mouth opened. She snapped it shut. "I can't believe it. You want me to be your secretary?"

He let out a quick sigh. "And my partner's. I actually had my interview with you last night without you being aware of it. You'd mentioned what your old boss said in her glowing reference letter for you. And Tom, my partner, always leaves these administrative decisions up to me. So...do you want the job?"

She bit her lower lip and stared at him, wide-eyed.

"Alanna? I thought you'd be happy to get the job offer."

"I am. Sorry. It's a surprise, that's all. I do want the job."

"Outstanding. I know you'll fit in well with the staff. Do you want to meet them? Since tomorrow's Thanksgiving and we're closed for the rest of the week, you won't start until Monday. But you can get the new employee paperwork out of the way today unless you have somewhere else to go."

After a long exhale, Alanna beamed. "I've nowhere else to be. I'd love to meet everyone."

They drained their cups and left the coffee shop. Two minutes later, they walked through the front door of the Fairbrook Clinic. Several patients, magazines in hand, dotted the waiting room's nicely-upholstered seats.

Chris leaned over and whispered, "Most of our patients arrive early."

She nodded.

They stepped into the front office area, and Chris introduced Alanna to Angel, the receptionist. She looked so young. *Must be a recent high school graduate.* They proceeded down a hall of closed examination rooms. "Are the rooms full?"

"No. On Wednesday and Friday, we start an hour later than the rest of the week. Ten o'clock. But we work through lunch, taking turns with breaks. And we close at three on Friday, so our staff can start their weekend early."

What terrific hours. Much better than the hospital where she'd worked.

They neared the end of the hall. "This past week, we decided to close on Saturdays instead of Wednesdays. Everyone seemed thrilled." He snickered.

She followed Chris to the lab at the rear of the building. "Ladies, I'd like you to meet Alanna McCarthy, our new medical secretary, starting Monday morning."

Three nurses gave her their attention and smiled.

Chris held out his hand toward the nurse closest to Alanna. "This fiery redhead is Rebecka."

The tall, shapely woman with brilliant green eyes thrust her hand out to Alanna. "Becka for short. Welcome. I'm thrilled you're here. The doctors have been lost without a secretary." She chortled.

The next nurse, Tess, according to her name tag, had short brown hair and honey-colored eyes. Her wide grin revealed slight buckteeth. She didn't wait for Chris to introduce them. "Glad you're joining us, girl. I'm Tess."

The last of the nurses held back. Chris bent his finger, motioning her forward. "Alanna, this quiet lady is Melanee. But don't let her fool you. She's a tyrant when a patient gets out of line." He chuckled.

Melanee blushed and giggled, then held out her hand. "Nice to meet you, Alanna. Welcome to Fairbrook." With her pixie-cut hair and sparkling powder blue eyes, she reminded Alanna of a blonde-haired elf. So cute. Missing the pointed ears, though.

Alanna shook Melanee's hand. "Thank you." The three nurses resembled a staircase, equally spaced in height, with Melanee the bottom step at under five feet and Becka the top at almost six. "I'm happy to meet all of you."

Chris turned to leave, and Alanna followed him through another hall. He stopped at the first door. "This will be your office."

What a spacious room, with a nice large window. White vertical blinds opened to a view of the landscaped side of the building. A dark walnut desk with a floor-to-ceiling bookcase full of manuals behind it sat on a deep blue carpet. "Beautiful."

On the other side of hers, they entered Chris's office with a desk in front of wall-to-wall bookcases, filled with medical books and journals. An old football on a stand, a doctor figurine with a large stethoscope, pictures— obviously from college days—and other memorabilia filled the nooks and crannies. A plaque at eye level caught her attention. "So, you're a Navy-trained doctor."

"That I am, young lady. Spent most of my time with the Marines, though. Oorah!"

She giggled as she viewed the three remaining walls of dark walnut paneling, which complemented the bookcases. That would make Chris a little older than Jake had been, counting his training and the service dates indicated on the plaque.

They moved on, and he stopped in the doorway of the next office. A man whose linebacker physique stretched his lab coat to the limit stood to greet them. His youthful face contradicted his white hair.

"Tom, meet our new secretary, Alanna McCarthy. She starts on Monday. Alanna, this is my partner, Thomas Jeffries, M.D."

Dr. Jeffries rounded the desk, eying Chris. "So you found another Irishman to fill the office and gang up on me, huh?" The man punched Chris in the arm and turned to Alanna. His lips spread across his face in a wide smile as he shook her hand in a tight, firm grasp. "Welcome to Fairbrook Clinic, Alanna." He returned to his desk.

"Thank you, Doctor Jeffries. I'm pleased to be here."

Alanna couldn't get over the shock of white hair on the gentleman. She dragged her eyes away and peered up at Chris.

As they continued down the hall, he whispered close to her ear. "He comes by that mop of white hair honestly. He's my age, but the men in his family all have white hair by the time they're thirty. It gives people a jolt when they see him. It's so...*white*."

"It's dramatic." She covered a giggle with her hand. "Is he Navy-trained too?"

"No. Civilian. He took over his father's practice while I was in the service. When I got out, he offered me a partnership. We'd gone to school together from kindergarten all the way through college. Great guy."

They approached the next door, and he pointed with his thumb. "Mandy's our office manager. She's been doing the HR work, although she'll delegate those duties to you. I should have told you that before asking if you wanted the job."

"No problem, Chr— I'd better get used to calling you Doctor Maguire from here on. HR duties are no problem. I helped out in Human Resources in the hospital, and I'd rather be busy than bored."

"Okay." He opened Mandy's door, and the scent of oranges floated into the hall. "Mandy, you've been eating oranges for breakfast at your desk. Haven't you?"

A short, plump, middle-aged woman with tightly-curled brown hair that reached to her earlobes chortled. "You betcha, doc. And they were good ones too."

A path of freckles trailed across her cheeks and the bridge of her nose. Her hazel eyes glowed under the fluorescent lighting above her desk.

The woman grinned at Chris, then at Alanna. "This must be our new employee, Alanna McCarthy."

Alanna shook her offered hand. "Yes, ma'am."

"Please, don't call me ma'am. I'm plain old Mandy around here. I don't want to be your mama. We're all friends here at the clinic. The doctors are the ones who get called by a title. At least here in the office." She winked at Chris.

"Yes, ma—Mandy. Sorry. I was raised to say ma'am to those in authority, so it'll take getting used to."

"Okay. I won't call you out on it. Are you here to simply meet the crew, or do you have time for your paperwork? Either is fine with me."

"I have plenty of time...if I'm hired."

"Of course you are. After Doctor Maguire told me about you, and I read that letter of recommendation, I was convinced you were the right one for the job."

Alanna let out a sigh of relief. What a grand feeling. Hired. She had a job. And what a job, what a place, and what a— She glanced at Chris.

The same thought that troubled her when Chris asked if she wanted the job hit her. They'd work together. Her for him. There'd be no chance for a relationship with this wonderful man now. Her heart crashed.

Chapter Nine

Chris accompanied Alanna from the clinic back to her car in the coffee shop parking lot once she completed her new-employee paperwork. This beautiful woman would cross his path every day at work from here on. With her beauty, crystalline green eyes, long strawberry-blonde hair, and a shape to rival any model, the love bug sure had hit him fast. Not to mention, she was a ten on the personality scale. But to bond in such a short time. With Sheila, it had taken all through high school and college. He'd have to thank Susie and Marmalade for finding Alanna.

When they reached her car, Chris touched Alanna's arm. "May I take you out to dinner tonight to celebrate your new job?"

Her brows puckered as she stared at his hand. "Do you take every new employee out for dinner?"

"No. Why?"

A deep shade of pink flowed into her cheeks. She pressed her lips shut.

Uh oh. Had she thought he expected special privileges from her for offering the job? He dropped his hand to his side. Did she feel harassed? "Alanna, I didn't mean...you don't owe me." Bad way to start. He had to fix this fast.

She retrieved her keys from her purse and looked up. "Doesn't the clinic have rules regarding employee relationships?"

"We've never wanted to interfere with any of our employees' lives. What they do, who they date, is their business unless it affects the clinic. You having dinner with me as my friend is personal."

Chris winced. "If you'd rather we didn't date, it's okay. But we started off so well, and I wanted to help you celebrate. If I made you uncomfortable, I'm sorry." His heart shrank. He drew in a cleansing breath.

A smile formed on Alanna's mouth. "I misunderstood. It's just that I've heard of bosses who expect things from their employees other than what's in the job description. I shouldn't have jumped to the wrong idea." She lowered her lashes. "Jake used to say I had an uncanny sense when it came to judging a person's character. My first impression of you was what I should have stuck with. That you're honest and trustworthy."

"I hope you will."

She nodded. "Susie and Marmalade made it easier for me. The way they act around you." She unlocked the driver's side.

His heart lifted. He opened the door and held it while she slid behind the steering wheel.

She gazed up at him.

Chris bent over, resting his arms on the top of the open door. "So, may I take you out to dinner tonight to celebrate?"

"Yes. I suppose we can keep our friendship separate from our work relationship."

"Sounds like a wise idea. Mexican or Italian food...or what?"

"Mexican sounds good to me. Haven't had it for a while."

As she looked off to his right, her smile drooped, and a worried expression took its place. He followed her line of sight to a light-haired man who glared at him through the open window of a red Camaro. The man pulled out of the far-corner parking space and sped into the street.

Chris turned back to Alanna when she started the engine. "Do you kno—?"

"I'd better get home and take Susie out. She didn't spend much time on business this morning, and I'm sure she's getting uncomfortable." Alanna closed the car door.

Chris allowed it to click shut.

Her eyes met his as she rolled down the window. "When should I be ready tonight?"

"Is six okay? It'll give me time to clean up when I leave here." Why did she interrupt his question?

"Thank you, Chris." When she smiled, his pulse kicked into high gear. He backed away from the car, and she drove away.

As he entered the clinic, his thoughts returned to the man in the Camaro. Who was he? Someone she knew, no doubt? But her facial expression said she wasn't pleased to see him. A former boyfriend?

Alanna parked in her driveway and turned off the engine. Why had Steve been at The Hot Brew? She slipped out of the car.

Steve's red Camaro screeched to a stop at the end of the driveway. He jumped out and rushed up to Alanna. "Who was that guy you were with? You won't give me the time of day, but you'll run around with him when you're supposed to be looking for work?" He stopped inches behind her.

She slammed the car door shut and faced him. "What are you doing here? Where do you get off speaking to me in that tone? And what is it to you what I was doing or who I was with?"

He backed off, took his hands off his hips, and lowered his arms. After a huff, he grimaced. "Sorry. I was out of line. I've tried so hard to get you to go out with me. When I saw your car at the coffee shop, I decided to join you. When you weren't inside, I figured you were at the clinic next door applying for work, so I waited to ask if you'd have lunch with me. Then you walked out with that guy. Always did have a jealous streak. I'm sorry."

"You're not my boyfriend, Steve. Let's drop it and move on."

"But who is he? The way he leaned over your car door—"

"Drop it, Steve."

He frowned. "Guess a doctor's more your type. But who is he?"

"I met the doctor when I found his lost pets. He needed a secretary. But none of this is your business. Please go, and leave me alone. I don't need any more help. And you should find someone who wants your attention."

Steve stared at the front window of her house.

Alanna turned. Susie and Marmalade were on the back of the couch at the window with their heads stuck between the sheer curtains. Susie barked. Marmalade flattened her ears against her head. The curtains moved as if in an approaching storm.

Steve spun, stomped back to his car, and sped off.

As she walked across the stepping stones to her front door, she shivered. Something told her this wasn't the last episode with the flamboyant and persistent Steve Brennan.

Chapter Ten

C hris drove to his favorite upscale Mexican restaurant, Tabla Alejandro, while Alanna sat quietly in the passenger seat. What a treat to have yet another dinner with the gorgeous Alanna. He could get used to this. Plus, she'd promised to have him over for a home-cooked meal soon.

He glanced at her. She gazed through the windshield as if a hundred miles away. Why? "Alanna, are you okay? You're very quiet."

She turned to him and smiled.

Dazzling smile. No wonder he was falling in love with her.

"I'm fine. I thought of something that happened earlier."

"Suzie? Marmalade? They didn't—"

"No." She laughed. "They were as good as gold. Not one mess anywhere, of any kind. A visitor stopped by when I got home from the clinic. He upset them. They've not acted like that before."

"Let me guess. Red Camaro guy?"

She nodded and looked at her folded hands.

"I had a hunch he was trouble. What happened?" He reached his hand to touch hers. "I don't mean to pry."

"It's okay."

Chris maneuvered the car around a busy corner. "He glared at me when I turned to see what you were staring at before you left the coffee shop parking lot. When he drove off, it was in the opposite direction you took."

"And yet, he wound up at my house right behind me."

"Is he harassing you, threatening in any way? Did you report him to the police?"

Alanna bit her bottom lip.

He loved that little quirk of hers. She looked so cute. Chris tilted his head, waiting for an answer.

Her eyes narrowed. "He's not a threat to me. When I worked at the hospital, I'd run into him in the halls. He introduced himself in the cafeteria one day. Sat at my table as if I'd invited him." She paused.

Chris huffed. "Some guys assume they have special privileges when it comes to women."

"Well, he never struck me that way. But after he'd introduced himself, he'd run into me, here, there, and everywhere. In the hall, the cafeteria, parking lot. It was as if he had radar tuned into me. Each time, he'd ask me to go out with him, and I'd refuse." She sighed. "When I was laid off, he started calling. How he got the number, I have no idea. Maybe from his friend in HR."

Chris clenched his jaw. "Some people also have ways of getting information they shouldn't, when they're determined enough."

Alanna nodded.

"So, he keeps calling you?"

"So often I had to block him. It was him at The Hot Brew today. But he's never been mean, or downright rude. No ruder than a lot of men I've run into, anyway. Only obnoxious. Which is how he acted at the house. He demanded to know who you were."

When they arrived at the restaurant, Chris parked the car and turned off the engine. He faced Alanna and reached across the console for her hand. "Are you sure he's not stalking you?"

A glimmer of a smile showed on her face. "Don't worry, Chris. Steve merely has trouble taking no for an answer. He gets bent out of shape."

"Men who can't take no for an answer can be dangerous."

She shifted in her seat, and her white shawl slipped behind her, revealing her forest green dress, which made the emerald green of her eyes deep and mysterious. It was no wonder Camaro guy was infatuated with her.

"Steve doesn't strike me as dangerous. What I said to him today should be sufficient to make him leave me alone."

"Why not let me talk to him? Where does he work in the hospital?"

Alanna's jaw dropped. "Talk to him?" This could cause more trouble. "Let me tell you what happened. Steve drove up as I pulled into my driveway. He accused me of not giving him a chance and spending time with you when I needed to find a job. It sounded ridiculous. But he's not dangerous."

Chris squeezed her hand and shook his head.

"I told him it was none of his business what I did. Then he apologized." She retrieved her hand from Chris's clasp and held out both palms up. "It's nothing to worry over. He admitted he was out of line. I told him you were *only* my new boss."

Only her new boss?

She covered her mouth and giggled. "Susie and Marmalade got in the front window and showed him how upset *they* were with him. I asked him to leave, and he did. Does that sound like something I need to report to the police?"

"I guess not." Chris opened the driver's door and got out of the car. He strode to the passenger side and opened the door for Alanna. He was working toward something much more than *only her boss.* And he didn't trust this Steve guy.

As he held her hand in his, another tingle surged up his arm. He wanted to protect her, make sure nothing ever hurt her. "Let's get inside and eat before these hungry Houstonians deplete the food supply."

As they waited for their fajitas, Alanna gazed at Chris's handsome face. Every butterfly in Harris County must be captive in her stomach and chest, fighting to be set free. *What this man does to me with one look should be illegal.*

"Chris, I've answered all your questions about my life, but I haven't had a chance to ask you anything about yours."

"Have I monopolized every conversation?"

"You did allow me to answer your questions." She chortled. "But now it's my turn to ask."

"Okay, shoot." He leaned back in the chair and crossed his arms over his chest.

His sports coat did little to conceal his well-developed muscles. *He sure is a hunk.* Her sister's voice sounded in her mind. *"Ack, Ally, is dat any way to speak of a gentleman?"* A giggle slipped out.

He tilted his head.

"Okay, Doctor Maguire, before we left the house, you told me you became a doctor because you wanted to take care of people, diagnose their problems, and administer the correct cure. But why is this handsome young doctor unattached?"

Sadness filled his eyes, and he sat forward.

Too personal? She'd never had a knack for this small talk stuff. "Forgive me. I shouldn't have asked."

"If anyone else had, I'd have changed the subject."

"Chris, I'm sorry." She reached for his hand, resting on the table.

He took hers in his. "It's okay. I'm comfortable talking to you."

The waiter brought their fajitas. Alanna's mouth watered from the aroma of steak, peppers, and onions. "That smells so good."

"Aha. A reprieve."

"Not for long, doctor. You can talk between bites."

He winked at her and prepared his first tortilla.

A few minutes later, he gazed at Alanna. "I was married."

"You were?" Her heart jolted. "But you're not now? Is that what you mean?"

"Right. Sheila and I dated throughout high school and college. We married while I was in the service. Before our first anniversary, we had a little boy...Scott. He was a blessing. My family said he resembled me as a child."

As Chris's eyes glistened, Alanna's heart tore.

He blinked tears away. "Before his second birthday, Scott died from a rare disease. Sheila was devastated. So was I. By then, I had discharged and managed to throw my emotions into my work, but I wasn't strong enough to help both of us. She said she needed space and moved out."

"Oh, Chris. You don't have to go on."

He smiled. "I've never wanted to tell anyone this before. But I want to tell you."

She glanced at an older couple sitting nearby who stared at Chris. Alanna squeezed his hand. "Okay, but we should eat our dinner, then go back to my house for coffee. You can finish in private."

"You're right. That'd be a better place to talk."

Would he tell her what happened with Sheila? Was he still in love with his   ex-wife?

Chapter Eleven

*A*fter dinner, Chris and Alanna returned to her house. He hung his sports coat on the rack in the foyer and headed to the couch. Susie and Marmalade snuggled next to him, the cat purring as loud as ever. "Sure have missed you guys. I'll be happy when it's my turn to have you." He glanced into the kitchen, where the sounds of coffee preparation filtered out. "Do you need any help in there?"

"No, thank you. I can handle it."

He had a hunch she'd handle most anything. "Yell if you change your mind."

"Actually..."

He laughed. Just like a woman. "I knew it had to be too good to last." He sprang from the sofa and strode into the kitchen.

When he came up behind Alanna, she jumped and faced him. "What are you wearing, silencers on your feet?"

Inches from her, he resisted the urge to kiss her as his heart pounded like a bass drum. "Ah...I thought you needed help." He took a step back. *Whoa.* What happened? *Slow down, buddy.*

"Now that I'm here, what can I do?" Get his emotions under control for one thing. It must be those enchanting green eyes. One look and he was under a spell.

"Okay. Um. Let me see."

Had she felt the magnetism between them too? He took a deep breath and blew it out slowly as he continued to fight the urge to cover her lips with his. Her cheeks turned red. She must sense his struggle.

Alanna spun back to the counter. "Would you mind getting the cream from the refrigerator? I'll get out a creamer. Oh, but it's two percent milk, I hope you don't mind. I don't use cream. Oh, you already know that."

He smiled and stepped to the refrigerator. As nervous as a cat in a room full of rockers. Maybe more so than him.

By the time the coffee was ready, Alanna had set mugs, utensils, creamer, and the sugar bowl on a rolling cart, and Chris's pulse had moderated. A minute later, she loaded the carafe, napkins, and two plates with a slice of white frosted chocolate cake on each onto the cart. He added the forks.

Chris rolled the coffee cart into the living room and parked it at the side of the couch. "How come you got a bigger slice than I did?" His mouth made a frown.

Alanna pointed at the double-portioned plate. "That one's for you, as if you hadn't guessed."

He laughed and picked up his plate.

She shook her head and lowered herself onto the unoccupied end of the sofa. "So, do you want to talk more? What happened to Scott? If you prefer not to speak of it, I'll understand. My heart aches for what you've gone through, although I've not had the blessing of a child. Jake and I wanted to wait until we were better off financially, but..."

The moisture welling in her eyes tore at Chris's heart. She mourned not having her own child as much as he mourned the loss of Scott. He stood and reseated himself beside her, placing his plate back on the table. He stretched his arm around her shoulders and drew her to his side. A tear slid down her cheek and fell to his shirt. "You'll have your chance to be a mom, and I'll bet you'll be a fantastic one." Hopefully, he'd be a part of it. *Wow, talk about rushing things.*

She gazed up at him and smiled. "I love kids."

Susie jumped down from the cushions and back up on the other side of Alanna, squeezing herself into the space next to the armrest. The dog licked Alanna's arm as if she sympathized with her. Marmalade hopped onto the back of the sofa and padded behind Chris to rub her head against Alanna's ear.

Chris chuckled. "*These kids* are great, though, aren't they?"

As she nestled her head onto his shoulder, Alanna whispered, "They are."

He pulled her closer. His pulse raced. He'd better get his mind on something else. "I'll tell you the rest of the story while we have our coffee."

Alanna laid her hand on his arm. "If you want to. It has to hurt to bring it up."

"I think it would do me good to tell you what happened." He rested his head on hers. "As far as Scott goes, there's not much more to tell. We had the funeral. Sheila and I tried to resume our lives. The comfort I had...*have*...is knowing I'll see him in heaven someday. He's with our Lord. No more pain, no sickness, running around on streets of gold, singing praises to God at the top of his lungs." He chuckled. "He always loved to sing. The little guy sang hymns all day—in his own way."

"What a marvelous memory to hold onto."

"Yes. Those thoughts helped me through the next part." He missed Scott so much. But God knew what was best. "Sheila moved out and dove into her career as a real estate agent. She filed for divorce, citing insupportability, or irreconcilable differences, whatever that's supposed to mean. What it meant was, she didn't want to try to work things out between us. But with Scott gone, I had no desire to contest."

He stopped for a minute to take a deep breath. "What I thought we had through those years in school and the beginning of our marriage had vanished. Could be it was never there in the first place. Neither of us had siblings, so we'd clung to each other. And our little boy was the glue that kept us together. But when we lost him, everything fell apart. That's what I think happened."

Tears rolled over Alanna's cheeks. He took the mug from her hands and set it on the table. With his right hand, he stroked her cheek while he wiped away the drops with his thumb. "Sorry I made you cry."

From the end table, she snatched a tissue from the box and wiped her eyes. "It's okay. We've both suffered a terrible loss. It's hard to lose a loved one and go through loneliness so deep inside it aches. Jake was the only man I'd ever loved. Outside of my da, that is."

The strong urge to kiss her returned. He removed his arm from around her, sat up straight, and picked up his coffee. *Control...control.* After a sip, he lowered the cup to the table.

"So, Sheila never came back?"

"No. And I'm ashamed to say, it never bothered me. I moved on. Concentrated on my practice. Dated on rare occasions over the past year, but never the same woman twice. No one had interested me." *Until now.*

He turned to face Alanna and found her staring at his lips as if mesmerized. He lowered his to hers, and his arms encircled her. As their heads tilted in opposite directions, he deepened the kiss.

Her fingers feathered through his hair until one hand clenched a lock on the back of his head. He pulled away, and she dropped her hand to her lap. Out of breath, he stared at her. His jaw dropped as he gulped in a breath.

She panted, and her eyes widened.

"Alanna. I'm sorry. I shouldn't have done that." He stood and hurried toward the door.

As Chris grabbed his sports coat and strode to the door, Alanna jumped to her feet. "It's my fault, Chris. I'm the one who should be sorry. Please, forgive me."

He turned. "Sorry for what? I kissed you."

"But I kissed you back and latched onto you like a drowning cat." She looked at the floor where the pets sat doing their pendulum routine. Were they as confused as she was? Was it guilt for betraying Jake she felt?

He walked back to her and grasped her shoulders. "We've both been lonely this past year." He picked her chin up with his hand until she looked into his eyes. "I don't regret that kiss, as long as you don't. It felt good."

She smiled. Those dratted butterflies. "It was...wonderful."

He drew her to his chest and wrapped his arms around her. "But perhaps, under the circumstances, we'd better call it a night. Our emotions are running high."

"Yes. A good idea." She closed her eyes and nodded. Her head swam from his cologne, cedar trees in winter. *So nice.*

They walked hand-in-hand to the front door. The cat and dog followed and then sat behind Alanna on either side.

He faced her and pulled her hand to his lips, kissing her fingers. "Goodnight, dear Alanna. Thank you for the coffee and...sweets."

She jumped back. "Your cake! You didn't get to eat it. Or finish your coffee. Wait there a minute." She ran to the table in the living room, swooped up his plate and cup, and sprinted to the kitchen, the animals on her heels.

Alanna pulled out a storage container from the cabinet, slid the piece of cake into it, and added a second slice. She took her travel mug from the drainer, poured his coffee into it, and secured the lid. She rushed back to him and pushed the mug and container toward him. "Don't try to eat it on the way home." She giggled. "The coffee, okay. Not the cake."

"Yes, Mother."

They laughed.

Chris bent to give each furry kid a pat on the head and then slid his hand to the back of Alanna's neck. He gave her a warm and delicious kiss before he opened the door. "Sweet dreams. Thank you for the cake, and the use of your mug. It's been a long time since I had such a terrific evening. You are special." He lifted the cup. "I'll see that this gets back to you."

She rose on her tiptoes, gave him a quick kiss on the corner of his mouth, and stepped away. Warmth filled her neck. "Thank you for dinner."

She smiled. "And...everything." A tingle traveled through her body as heat flooded her face.

Without another word, he stepped out the door and pulled it closed with a solid click.

Chapter Twelve

hris strode to his car and slid behind the wheel. "Wow!" He inserted the key and started the engine. He glanced back at the house. *Wow.* Alanna, Susie, and Marmalade gazed out the window. Alanna waved. "Wow!" He waved and pulled out of the driveway.

As he drove away, his mind stayed on the kisses they'd shared. He'd never fallen so hard for any woman, not even Sheila. His heartbeat sped into overdrive. One month after he'd met her and—

He glanced at the rearview mirror as he turned the first corner. A red car followed. *Camaro guy?*

At the next corner, the red car turned. Sure looked like a Camaro. Although, that Steve guy didn't have the only red Camaro in town. Strange coincidence, though.

Chris turned at the next block and drove back toward Alanna's to make sure the suspicious Camaro didn't show up there. If it did, Camaro guy was in big trouble. As Chris turned the last corner on Alanna's block, he checked the cross street. No red Camaro. He drove by her residence. The lights were off. Must have been a false alarm.

As he headed home, his thoughts returned to the sweet kisses he and Alanna had shared. He'd have to be cautious at work not to show the growing affection he had for her. But it'd be hard. *Yep, man. You've fallen.* No use denying it. He was so wrapped up in her, he forgot to say happy Thanksgiving.

There was no doubt the emotion was real on his part, no matter how fast it had happened. But was Alanna over Jake? Ready to move on? Her responses might be a reaction to her loss and loneliness. He had to be careful. Having another broken heart was not on his agenda.

Alanna lay fully clothed on her bed. What had he meant by he'd see that her cup got back to her? Wouldn't he bring it back? She'd forgotten to wish him a happy Thanksgiving. But then, he'd not mentioned tomorrow either. Probably has plans. Susie curled up on one side of her, Marmalade purring on the other.

Her heart still raced from the kisses she and Chris had shared. How would she sleep? How could this have happened? She'd never kissed anyone like that. Jake's face visualized in the growing darkness of the room.

She rolled onto her side and squeezed the pillow with both hands. Had she truly fallen in love with Chris? It hadn't been a year since Jake passed. She'd met Chris a month ago. She couldn't be in love already, could she?

A minute later, she swung her legs over the edge of the bed and slipped out to the living room. She sat on the sofa where she'd been sitting when Chris kissed her. The tingle traveled through her again. *Oh, God, what's happening to me?*

She should read The Psalms. Jake always said to read The Psalms when something troubled her. Would they calm her?

Alanna raced to the bookshelf, pulled out her Bible, and sat in the armchair. After another glance at the couch, she pulled the afghan around her shoulders and opened the book to Psalm 143. *Please, let it help.* She read through verses three and four, paused, and reread.

"For the enemy hath persecuted my soul; he hath smitten my life down to the ground; he hath made me to dwell in darkness, as those that have been long dead. Therefore is my spirit overwhelmed within me; my heart within me is desolate." That was exactly what happened to her when Jake died. What had been happening for the last year...until Chris came along. Now what?

She continued reading. At verse eight, she stopped for a moment, then read it a second time aloud.

"Cause me to hear thy lovingkindness in the morning; for in thee do I trust: cause me to know the way wherein I should walk; for I lift up my soul unto thee." This was her prayer. She needed guidance. "God, what do You want me to do? Are You there?" It was easy feeling the way she did for Chris, but should she? What if he really loved his ex-wife, and was simply angry with her for leaving? *If I give him my heart, and Sheila comes back—*

"God, I need You to take control of my emotions. Of Chris's emotions. Help us."

Chapter Thirteen

The following Monday morning, Alanna entered the clinic to start her new job. She hadn't seen Chris since last Wednesday night. Not since those passionate kisses they'd shared. Relentless butterflies swarmed in her stomach. She had to put on her professional face and keep it when she ran into him. And remember to refer to him as Doctor Maguire. Better get that name planted in her mind.

She hurried through the hall, past Chris's closed office door. Odd. He'd told her he closed his door during a private consultation, but his first patient wasn't scheduled for another hour. Maybe he had a private phone call. It'd give her more time to psych herself into thinking of him as no more than her boss. *Right.*

Doctor Maguire may have spent Thanksgiving somewhere else and hadn't returned yet. That would account for the door being closed. Congratulations, Alanna. She actually remembered to call him Doctor Maguire instead of Chris.

When she arrived at Mandy's office near the end of the hall and stepped through the doorway, the supervisor greeted her with a smile. "Good morning, Alanna. Ready to start?"

"I am."

Mandy motioned for Alanna to take the chair next to her desk. "The secretary's work has backed up since Janet's accident."

Alanna's brows furrowed. "Janet?"

"The clinic's secretary for the past five years. She was in a car wreck and suffered serious injuries. She's on disability now."

"I'm sorry to hear that. But I thought you had another girl take her place for a while. Why is everything so backed up?"

"We did. When we found out Janet wasn't coming back, we found a girl who worked out for the first week. But she was more interested in telling everyone how to do their job than doing hers. The doctors said she'd have to go."

Mandy stood and rounded her desk. "I started a new search right away but didn't find a suitable match for our office. Not until the day Doctor Maguire mentioned you. I'm glad he found you."

"I am too, Mandy." *I am too.* Alanna smiled.

Mandy led Alanna to the break room. "I'm aware the doctor showed you around last Wednesday, but I want to make sure he covered everything. Care for a cup of coffee to take with you as we go on tour?" She pointed to the cup hangers on the wall. "These are clinic mugs, but you're welcome to bring in your own if you prefer."

Before Alanna responded, Mandy stretched up for a mug and handed it to Alanna.

Alanna stifled a giggle. *Obviously, a true coffeeholic and thinks everyone else should be too. This was going to be a great job.*

After filling the mug, Alanna followed Mandy out of the break room. When they got to her office, Mandy grabbed her cup from the desk and continued down the hall to Dr. Jeffries' office. A newspaper spread out across his desk.

The office supervisor tapped on the physician's doorframe, and he glanced up. "Good morning, Doctor Jeffries. Alanna is starting today. Do you have anything you want her to do?"

"Good morning, Mandy, Alanna." He gave her his broad smile and turned to Mandy. "Nothing at the moment. She has enough piled on her desk for now. Hope we don't overload her."

Alanna shook her head. "I'll be fine, sir. I'd rather be busy than not."

"Good attitude. You'll be an asset to our team here. And don't worry, you'll be plenty busy. At least for a while."

"Thank you, sir."

When they reached Chris's office, his door was open, but the room was empty.

"Doctor Maguire's a real go-getter." She pointed her thumb at his office and then turned to Alanna. "Like you." Mandy laughed. "You'll get along great."

Warmth traveled through Alanna's neck and into her face. *Think about something else.* She'd have to run home at lunch and check on Susie and Marmalade, alone in the house.

The first half-day on the job had gone without a hitch for Alanna. She'd fallen in easily with the office and clinic routine. Not that much different from what she did at the hospital. And what a pleasant staff. Especially Mandy. So easygoing.

The downside had been not seeing Chris. There. She'd done it again. *Doctor Maguire.* Though Mandy said they'd known each other for years, she called him doctor in the office.

Wait a minute. He'd have told Mandy he was going to be gone. Wouldn't he? She hadn't said anything.

Alanna grabbed her purse from the bottom desk drawer and trekked to the parking lot. She drove home to have lunch with her pets. How convenient to work fifteen minutes from the house. Susie'd appreciate being let out at lunchtime each day, even if she had been used to Chris's long hours away from the apartment.

Chris. Would they be able to work on a good relationship and keep their private life separate from the office? She hoped so.

On the way to the house, the kiss they'd shared replayed in her mind. It gave her goosebumps and set the dratted butterflies loose. Maybe it was a good thing she hadn't seen him all morning. It would give her time to get used to the idea of seeing him every day, and the little antagonists would settle down. So far, every time Chris had stepped into view, they'd taken flight.

Alanna pulled into the driveway and turned off the engine. Would he call her tonight? She dragged her purse from the passenger seat over the center console. Before opening the car door, discomfort squelched the energized butterflies as she glanced in the rearview mirror. Steve's red Camaro had pulled in behind her. *What now?*

As he strode toward her, she hopped out and turned to face him.

"So how's your first day at work going, Babe?"

Babe? "I'm not your Babe. Why are you here? Aren't you working today?"

"I'm on vacation this week." He smirked. "Thought I'd spend time with you."

Alanna's jaw dropped. "*Me?* I told you I have no intention of dating you. No, Steve. You'll not spend time with me."

She turned to go to the house, but he caught her elbow. "Look, Alanna. I've been very patient with you." He pulled her into his arms. "We could have a lot of *fun* getting to know each other...*better.*"

"Let go of me." She jerked away, but he caught her around the waist and crushed her to his chest.

Susie jumped into the window, pushed the sheers aside with her nose, and barked. Marmalade stuck her head through the open curtain and walked the window ledge, tail swishing.

"Steve, if you don't leave me alone, I'll call the police. Leave!"

He let her go and glared.

Alanna rushed to the front door as she fumbled in her purse for the house key. She glanced back.

Steve narrowed his eyes at the pets in the front window, turned, and stomped back to his car. The Camaro screeched as he backed into the street, and the tires left black streaks on the pavement as he sped off.

Alanna released the breath she'd been holding while hoping he'd not push his way into the house. What had gotten into the man? He had never been that aggressive while she worked at the hospital. Annoying, yes, but not like today. Had it been alcohol she smelled on his breath? At noon? Mouthwash or cough syrup, maybe?

Oh well. He'd left and wouldn't bother her anymore since she'd told him she'd report him to the police. What if he had followed her into the house? A chill ran through Alanna. *What if he comes back?*

That night, Alanna couldn't sleep. She'd enjoyed her first full day on the job but still didn't know why Chris had never come back to the clinic. It wasn't her place to ask anyone, and Mandy never mentioned where he'd gone.

Chris had never given her his cell number. Why? The one time she'd called him was when he asked her to phone the clinic on the first day they'd met. And he'd called her only from the clinic. Never from home. They'd never exchanged emails either.

She tossed and turned. Susie and Marmalade left their own bed, hopped onto Alanna's, and curled at her feet. Marmalade purred for a while and then fell asleep.

At midnight, Alanna gave up trying to sleep. She entered the kitchen to fix chamomile tea and afterward shuffled into the living room. The sounds of traffic from the Beltway several blocks from her home were absent. Such a quiet night. She set the teacup on the coffee table, slumped into the armchair, and gazed at the couch where Chris had first kissed her.

After a sip of tea, Alanna lifted her Bible from the end table and laid it in her lap. Her fingers found Psalms. She read a few verses, but her mind was elsewhere.

Chris. Would he come back tomorrow? Not a word from him in six days.

The old familiar sense of loneliness assailed her. She took a deep breath and exhaled slowly. Her eyes burned, but she fought against the waterworks. *Why God? Why allow this man into my life and heart, and then let this happen?* There must be something wrong with her. Was it because of the kiss they shared? Or because she'd kissed him before he walked out the door? Had she scared him away?

God, I need Your help. She'd just come out of the depression from losing Jake and didn't want to go back there. Jake had always turned to the Scriptures for comfort and help. Would it help her too?

Alanna flipped through the thin white pages of her Bible until she came to Isaiah 41:10.

Fear thou not; for I am with thee: be not dismayed; for I am thy God: I will strengthen thee; yea, I will help thee; yea, I will uphold thee with the right hand of my righteousness.

As she began to close the book, the pages flipped to an underlined passage in 1 Corinthians 13:13 and stayed open.

And now abideth faith, hope, charity, these three; but the greatest of these is charity.

She placed the Bible on the coffee table and got on her knees. *Faith.* Could she have faith? "Thank You, God. You were always there with the Words Jake needed. I'm not sure what's happening between Chris and me if anything, but You do, don't You? If there's something I need to do, or not do, please make it clear to me. I'm sorry I haven't been very trusting of You as of late."

She waited. Her mind went blank. How was she supposed to pray? Should she ask for forgiveness because she'd been too bold? "God, I'm so confused. I need Your help. I do have faith. I think I do, but—"

Her eyes flooded. "Please, God. Help me out of this confusion."

Alanna rose and pulled a tissue from the box. She wiped her eyes, blew her nose, and returned to the bedroom. She slipped into bed and closed her eyes. Susie and Marmalade snored softly.

As she drifted off to sleep, Chris's smiling face appeared.

Chapter Fourteen

Tuesday morning, Alanna arrived at work twenty minutes early. No Malibu. He wasn't there. Mandy had said he was the first one to arrive at the clinic each day, even before she did.

Alanna entered the building. Should she ask Mandy where he was? Oh, that would be good. And have her face glow as if she'd been under a sunlamp? No. She'd have to be patient and wait for him to come in. Or someone to mention where he was. Or, for him to call her.

Why hadn't he called? He had her phone number.

Mandy's voice drifted into the hall from her office. "Yes, Sir. I'll tell him."

Who would she tell? Tell what? Chris? Alanna's pulse increased as she entered her own office and placed her purse in the desk drawer.

A second later, Mandy breezed in.

Finally.

"Good morning, Alanna. I'm sorry to have to dump this on you on your second day here, but I need your help. I'll be out of the office for the rest of the week because of a family emergency. I've laid out instructions for you, and everything should be self-explanatory. But I'll give you my personal cell number in case you run into a problem. Sorry about this."

Not what she expected. Alanna bit her lower lip. "It's okay. I don't mind, Mandy. I'm willing to learn new responsibilities whenever you need me. Hope the emergency isn't too serious."

"It might be. I don't have time to explain because I have to make travel arrangements and get my things together. I'll take off in a little while to accomplish that, but I'll be back later before I catch my flight. Come with me to my office, and I'll show you where things are."

Alanna followed Mandy to her office and sat across the desk from her. Would she tell her where Chris was?

Mandy handed her a binder with several sheets of paper in it. "Here are the instructions for the duties I want you to take care of while I'm gone. Take time to go over everything. If you have questions, ask me before I leave the office, or phone me. Okay?"

"Of course. Is there anything I can do to help you get ready?"

"I suppose I could transfer my calls to you."

Alanna nodded. Probably not a good time to ask where Chris was. She smiled to herself. Maybe he'd call, and when she answered, she'd find out what happened to him.

After pointing out things Alanna would need from her office, Mandy rummaged through her desk. "I put my cell in here somewhere."

"Is that it behind you on the credenza?"

The woman spun in her chair. "Yes. Thank you." As she turned back to Alanna, she blew a stream of air from her lips that lifted her dark brown curly bangs almost straight upward. "I'll make this up to you. I promise."

"Not necessary. I'm sorry you're so stressed. Let me know if there's anything else I can help with." Alanna rose from the chair.

"Thanks." Mandy spun back to the credenza and started searching through it.

On the way back to her office, Alanna's mind returned to Chris. She should forget about a relationship with the doctor. It was obvious he wasn't interested. That kiss meant nothing to him.

She slumped into her desk chair. It was too good to be true that she'd found another man as wonderful as Jake. The binder dropped to her desk. *Get your head in a better place. Concentrate on work.*

Her cell rang, and she jumped to dig it out of her purse. She pressed the key to connect. Her heart sank. Another robocall.

For the rest of the week, Alanna worked hard on her new duties at the clinic, plus those Mandy had assigned in her absence. But the week had dragged by.

Here it was Friday and no word from Chris. She'd love to shut off her cell. Too many robocalls and wrong numbers, but what if he called? Ma and Da would be beside themselves if they couldn't reach her. And there was no telling when Meg would decide she needed to give her little sister another pep talk or lecture on coming home to Ireland. Dear Meg. The thought tugged at her heart.

She needed to think of Chris only as her boss. Hadn't she told herself that earlier in the week? What good had it done?

Alanna glanced at the clock for the fifteenth time in the last fifteen minutes. All she wanted to do was get home and spend a quiet evening with Susie and Marmalade. "Humph!" Chris hadn't cared enough to find out how the pets he'd said he missed so much were doing. Was everything an act? The emotion he showed too? A way to make her fall for him and have a quick affair. Had he moved on to someone else when he realized she couldn't do that?

Guilt hit her as she left work, slid into her Honda, and pulled away from the parking lot. Her accusation made no sense. She glanced into the rearview mirror to check traffic behind her. Was she being unfair, since she had no idea what had happened to him? Mandy was so rattled Tuesday, she probably forgot to explain why Chris wasn't at work. *God, please let Chris call and let me know what happened to him...or help me forget him.*

Fifteen minutes later, Alanna pulled into her driveway. She drew her house keys from her purse, exited the vehicle, and trudged to the house. She was exhausted. When she opened the door and stepped inside, the darkened house was too quiet. She switched on the foyer light. Where were those two rascals? "Susie? Marmalade?" They'd always greeted her at the door when she'd returned home. The hair on the back of her neck rose.

"Susie! Marmalade! Where are you?" Her frantic voice seemed to echo in the silence.

Alanna searched the house, but the pets weren't there. "Don't tell me I forgot them outside when I returned to work after lunch." She ran to the back door. Closed, but unlocked. *That's strange.* She'd always locked it, even when she let Susie and Marm out. Her heart beat faster. She opened the door and called for them again. They didn't come.

Tears welled in her eyes, as she combed the yard, under the bushes, behind and inside the shed. Nothing. *Where are they?* Why had the back door been unlocked? Alanna sniffed and went inside.

As she hurried into the living room, her foot kicked a book partially hidden by the armchair. She picked it up. Something flew from the pages and landed at her feet. A business card. Alanna picked it up and wiped her eyes. "It's Chris's." A medical book. How long had this been here?

Alanna threw the book and card onto the couch. She sped to the back door, opened it, and examined the door jamb. Nothing. Didn't look as if someone had broken in. But, she'd never been the victim of a break-in. Why would someone break into her house, leave a medical book with Chris's card, and steal a dog and a cat?

She shut the door, fell to her knees, and wept. *Why take Susie and Marmalade?* The drops splattered the kitchen floor tiles.

After a moment, Alanna stood to grab a paper towel and wipe her face. She subdued the waterworks and bent to wipe the moisture from the floor. A piece of plastic stuck between the threshold and side molding caught her eye. She lifted it, and her brows pinched. The broken corner from a credit card? She'd read an article years ago that mentioned the use of credit cards to open locked doors. She'd been using the deadbolt at night. Should have used it during the day too.

The corner of the card must've broken off when the intruder had used it to open the locked door. She searched the card but found nothing to tell her who it belonged to. The piece of plastic disclosed only the first two numbers of the account and part of the bank's name.

Alanna grabbed her winter jacket and rushed out the door to search the neighborhood for Susie and Marmalade. Maybe they ran out when the stranger came in. She had to find them.

The engine revved, and she took off. Icy wind blew in through the open window as she called their names while she drove.

She searched every street in her subdivision, through neighboring Jersey Village, and the neighborhoods on the other side of hers. She drove home with a heart like lead. Her two sweet furbabies were out in the cold. Except, this time, it was colder at night than when she'd first found them huddled on the porch. *God, please protect them.*

The instant she entered the house, she phoned the Sheriff's Department. Between hitches in her sentences, while she cried, she told him what she'd found.

The deputy arrived, and Alanna showed him the piece of credit card she'd found at the back door. "I don't understand why anyone would want to break in here and take my pets." She wiped her eyes, but it did no good. More flowed.

"Miss, why don't you wait in the living room while we check things out? Is anything else missing besides your animals?"

"I—I don't think so. I was so worried about my dog and cat, I haven't noticed."

"Okay, you go ahead and search the house. See if something else may have been taken."

Alanna moved from room to room, but nothing else appeared to be gone. Only Susie and Marmalade. What would she tell Chris?

Chris. She bit her lip. How had his business card and book gotten in the house?

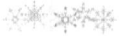

Through the night and into the wee hours of the next morning, Alanna tossed and turned with an unwelcome dream. By five a.m., she gave up trying to sleep. "May as well get out of bed." When she wasn't dreaming, her eyes were wide open. Either way, she wouldn't get any rest.

She threw her robe on and shuffled to the bathroom. "What a week." Had she done the right thing, telling the deputy she'd found Chris's card and book? He couldn't have done this.

Today, she'd call the animal shelters to see if Susie and Marmalade wound up there. Should make up more flyers too. Alanna burst into a crying jag. *Why is all this happening? What have I done to deserve this?* "Sure wish You'd simply tell me, God."

As Alanna stepped out of the shower, her mind replayed the dream that had tortured her through the night. The vision of a beautiful Sheila Maguire in Chris's arms. He'd never described her, but in her nightmare, Sheila had long, wavy black hair like his. They had embraced, leaving no question as to their desire for one another. In between passionate kisses, Sheila told Chris how sorry she was for leaving him. She wanted to come home.

Alanna shook the vision away and mopped her face. Was that God's way of telling her Chris could never be more than her boss?

Several minutes later, she dropped her uneaten egg and toast in the sink, ran water, and flipped on the garbage disposal. Alanna gulped a mouthful of hot liquid. The coffee had no more flavor than the eggs.

Better get busy. She collapsed into the chair at her desk and phoned the shelters. "Sorry, ma'am. No animals matching your pets' descriptions have been picked up or dropped off."

The receptionist's sympathetic words restarted Alanna's sobbing. "What should I do?"

"Miss McCarthy, email a copy of the flyer to us, and we'll upload it to our website. We've found and reunited many pets with owners this way. Have faith."

Alanna tried to smile. "Thank you. I'll send it as soon as I hang up."

She went to her file and found the picture Chris had taken of her hugging their dog and cat. Her brows furrowed. Chris couldn't have broken in and taken them. They'd be with him for this coming week anyway. But he may not have wanted to deal with questions about why he hadn't phoned her. What if he changed his mind and didn't want to share the pets? And what if Sheila had come back and didn't want him to share *anything* with another woman? He would've told his wife she had Susie and Marmalade.

The doorbell rang, followed by a knock.

Chris? She sprinted to the door and yanked it open.

"Hi, Alanna."

"Steve. What are you doing here again?" Should have checked the peephole first.

"I heard you lost your pets and thought I'd see if I could help you find them."

She didn't need this. Suspicion snaked through her. "How did you know my dog and cat were gone?"

"I have a friend in the Sheriff's Office. I happened to be chatting with her when the call came in."

He sure had a lot of convenient friends in convenient places. She narrowed her eyes at him. "I don't need your help. I've done everything there is to do."

"What about your new *boyfriend*. Is he helping you?"

"Boyfriend? If you're referring to my new boss, he doesn't even know they're missing." At least, she hoped he didn't know. He couldn't...wouldn't have done this.

"Look, Alanna. I'm sure you don't want to hear this, especially from me, but I've heard things concerning this guy. Bad things."

"What? What things?"

"When I mentioned his name to Alicia in HR at the hospital and that you got a job at his clinic, she made a face and said Doctor Maguire's name as if it were poison. I asked her why, and she said rumor had it that he caused his son's death. His wife left him because of it. Thought I'd tell you, so you don't get mixed up with him. She said he's a real ladies' man too."

"That's ridiculous. Chris—Doctor Maguire did not cause his son's death. There was nothing anyone could do. His wife left because of depression. Not that it's any of your business. This rumor needs to be stopped."

Steve glared, then cleared his throat. "Sorry to upset you. I just wanted to help."

Sure, you did. She needed to put an end to his contacting her once and for all. "I told you to leave me alone. I meant it. I told you I'd report you for harassment if you showed up. You either leave now, or I'll call the Sheriff's Department. No more stops at my house. No mailing me anything. And delete my email address. One more contact from you of any kind, and I'll file a restraining order against you. Do you understand?"

"You're gonna come crawling to me, Baby, when that guy dumps you the way he did his wife. You'll come crawling. Better yet—"

He grabbed Alanna and pushed her into the house, slamming the door shut behind them. Clutching a fistful of hair at the back of her head, Steve forced her lips onto his as he backed her into the living room. His breath reeked of alcohol.

She jerked her knee upward into his groin.

"Aaaahh" He let go of her, grabbed himself, and staggered backward.

Alanna fled out the back door and ran for the neighbor's house. Her heart jumped into her throat. No one would be there. They'd gone out of town for the weekend.

When the front door slammed, she peeked over the fence. Steve limped down the driveway toward his car.

Scrubbing her mouth with the back of her hand, Alanna ran through the back door and bolted it behind her. She rushed to the front door and turned the deadbolt. At the front window, she watched as the tires of the Camaro screeched down the street.

"Thank God." She clutched her hand to her chest and snatched a tissue to rub her mouth. It prickled from the way he had crushed his lips on hers. *"Crawling back to you," indeed. In your dreams.*

Should she call and report him? Would they believe her? He was gone, and no one saw what he did. They'd have come to help her if they had, wouldn't they? She closed the drapes on the front window. If he showed up again, she'd phone the Sheriff's Department and let them handle him.

Alanna braced a chair under the front doorknob and did the same to the back door. After her heart stopped pounding through her chest, she made a cup of tea and carried it to her computer. She entered her password and pulled up the flyer she'd saved from her previous search for Susie and Marmalade's owner. Glad she hadn't deleted it. She exchanged the original picture she'd taken of the pets with that of her hugging them and uploaded the new flyer to the list of missing pets on the shelters' sites. She'd print off a dozen sheets to hang up, too.

Her heart beat wildly. The voice of her family was what she needed at the moment. She phoned Meg. Voicemail clicked on after two rings. "Drat!" She must be working on a painting and turned off her cell. Alanna left a quick message for her sister to return the call and hung up.

Meghan would tell her she was ridiculous to get this upset over Susie and Marmalade. All their animals stayed outside. She should phone Ma and Da. They'd understand. They were always softhearted toward their animals on the farm. No. She couldn't tell them. She'd start to bawl, and they'd worry. Meg was the strong one. She'd give some supportive words, although she'd think her sister was foolish. Should she tell Meg about Chris?

Alanna checked the front of the house to make sure Steve's car wasn't within sight. All clear. She took a cup of coffee to the back porch. She had to relax before going out to post those flyers.

As she sat on the steps, tears filled her eyes. She'd quit her job and go back to Ireland. No more heartache. She couldn't take anymore or stay here and face daily reminders. The family wanted her home. Alanna set her cup on the step next to her and wrapped her arms around her knees.

First, she'd visit. Then she could decide. If Chris hadn't taken the animals, they'd be with him for the next two weeks...if she found them.

But there was her job to consider if she didn't move back to Ireland. She loved her new job. Could she get time off? She'd have to wait until Mandy got back. If she decided to stay in the States, she didn't want to risk losing her position at the clinic. But how would she work with Chris...after all this?

Chapter Fifteen

Saturday afternoon, Chris approached Alanna's street in his Malibu. His stomach had flip-flopped with anxiety for most of the drive back to Houston from Florida, wondering how Alanna liked her first week at work. She'd be surprised when he showed up on her doorstep.

What an idiot he'd been for not programming her number in his cell. He'd used the office phone each time he'd called her. Dumber to have left her number in his desk drawer at work and to never have given her his cell number. What had he been thinking? It was the last thing on his mind when he was with her or talked to her.

But why hadn't she gotten it from Mandy? Probably the same reason he hadn't gotten hers from Mandy after they'd decided to keep their relationship separate from work. At least she knew where he'd gone when Mandy or Tom told her.

Man, over a week without talking to Alanna. Torture.

Chris turned onto her street and parked in front of the house. He jumped out, hurried to the front door, and rang the bell as his pulse rate increased. No answer. She must be home. The Honda was in the driveway. He rang the bell a second time. Susie and Marmalade hadn't jumped into the window, either. They must be in the backyard.

He rushed over the stepping stones leading to the back gate. When he lifted the latch, his brows lowered at the sound of weeping. Chris rounded the house into the yard. Alanna sat on the back porch with her forehead pressed into her knees, her arms wrapped around her legs.

His heart lurched. "Alanna, what's wrong?"

She jerked her head toward him and gasped. *Chris?"* She swiped a sleeve across her tear-soaked face. "Where have you been? Susie and Marmalade...they're gone."

As he kneeled at her side, he collected her into his arms. "What do you mean they're gone? What happened?"

"They're missing."

He led Alanna inside and sat on the couch beside her. "Are you okay?" He dabbed at her cheeks with a tissue. "I'm so sorry I wasn't here for you." What a time to be needed in two places at once.

"What happened to you, Chris? I've been worried."

"Didn't Mandy or Tom tell you?"

"No one mentioned your name all week. When I came to work on Monday, your door was shut. Then it was open, but you weren't there. Things went crazy. On Tuesday, Mandy had to leave for a family emergency, and Doctor Jeffries had to juggle the patient load. Of course, I realized later that he must have gone into your office to retrieve the charts on your desk, but it was weird. Tess got sick on Wednesday and missed work for the rest of the week. It's been pandemonium."

He drew her to his chest and rubbed her back. "I'm sorry, Alanna. This has been a bad week for everyone." He lifted her chin with his finger. "My best friend Chet called me around midnight the Wednesday I last saw you. His father had a heart attack. Chet had been there for me through Scott's illness and death, and again when Sheila left. If he hadn't, I'd have lost my mind. So, I couldn't refuse to be there for him when he needed me. They live in Florida, and I left Thanksgiving day before sunrise. Fortunately, Chet's father recouped."

After Chris explained the misfortune with the phone numbers and why he hadn't gotten her number from Mandy, Alanna nodded. Waterworks spilled over her lower lashes and down her face. He brushed them away with his hand and reached for more tissues from the end table.

"I understand." Alanna straightened. "But what should we do about Susie and Marmalade? I don't know where they've gone."

She told him how she'd found the door unlocked and contacted the Sheriff's Office. "They said they'd investigate." She rose and paced the living room. "I made flyers. And phoned the shelters."

"Let's post the flyers." Chris stood and laid his hand on her shoulder. "Then we'll figure out if there's something else we can do."

Grabbing the flyers and her jacket, she dashed to the door but stopped before opening it. "Did you just get back from Florida?"

"Yes. Chet told me last night that his father would be okay. I left first thing this morning and drove straight through to get home."

Her hand stroked his stubbled chin. "I can do this myself. Why don't you stretch out on the couch until I get back? It won't take long. You have to be exhausted."

A tingle ran down his neck at her touch. "I'll go with you." He took the flyers from her hand. "When we finish posting these, we can stop to eat. I haven't eaten since dinner last night. Have you had lunch?"

"I tried to, but—"

Chris pulled her to his chest and kissed her. He stepped back. "I missed kissing you, but let's go. We'll see how far out we can get these." He clasped her hand and led her out the door to his car.

Guilt flooded Alanna for thinking Chris had taken Susie and Marmalade. Should she tell him? One thing she wouldn't reveal was the dream she'd had.

After they'd hung every flyer but one, Chris parked in front of a small diner.

Alanna glanced at him. "Aren't we going to post the last one?"

"Not yet. The Choo Choo Café has the greatest down-home country cooking if you don't mind it being right next to the railroad tracks. I'm starved. We eat first, and then we'll get a dozen more flyers made from this one." He pointed to the remaining paper in her lap. "We'll take them to neighborhoods farther out."

"That's a fabulous idea."

They entered the diner and took seats in a booth by the window. "Chris, I have a hunch."

He perused the menu. "What's that?"

"Susie and Marmalade wouldn't have run off. They've been so happy, it doesn't make sense. Even when I've opened the front door and walked down the steps to retrieve the newspaper, they'd sit in the open doorway and wait for me to come back."

He nodded. "Someone deliberately took them."

A plump, middle-aged waitress waltzed to the booth.

Chris looked up at her. "Ma'am, I realize it's way past lunchtime, but is it too late to order breakfast?"

"Not if y'all are hankerin' for it." She smiled at him.

Chris ordered eggs and bacon, orange juice, toast, and coffee.

She turned to Alanna. "And you miss?"

"Coffee and toast." Probably all her stomach could handle.

"Alanna." He tapped the menu. "You have to eat. I don't want you to get sick."

"Okay. Scrambled eggs."

The waitress grinned and left.

"Chris, I found something in the house yesterday."

His brows pinched together. "What?"

"A medical book...and your clinic business card."

His eyes widened. "What kind of medical book?"

"A medical dictionary. You didn't leave one at my house, did you? Is it possible the card fell out of your wallet?"

He shook his head. "Not likely. They're difficult to get out of the card holder. Where were they?"

"The book was on the living room floor halfway under the armchair. Almost as if someone wanted me to find it. The card must have fallen out from the pages when I picked up the book."

"Did you tell the deputy?"

"Yes. He asked if they were there before the animals disappeared. I told him I'd never seen them before. Then he asked me if the corner of a credit card I found on the floor at the back door might be from one of my cards, which it wasn't. Someone broke into the house. Yet nothing was missing except the animals."

"That's strange." Chris raised his eyebrows and whispered. "Sounds like a mystery movie." He pursed his lips.

"It does. But I'm beginning to see a solution to the mystery. I have an idea who broke into my place. Steve, the man I know from the hospital where I worked. He didn't take anything but Susie and Marmalade."

The waitress returned to their booth with two steaming cups of coffee and creamers. "Here ya go for a start, darlin's." She sauntered away to wait on two women at the next booth.

Alanna narrowed her eyes and stared out the window at the Saturday traffic whizzing by. She faced Chris. "I have a confession to make. After I found your card and the book, I wondered if you had taken Susie and Marmalade, changed your mind, and didn't want to explain, or something."

"You really thought I'd do that to you?"

The question pricked her heart. "I had no idea what to think when you didn't come to work last week, and I hadn't heard a word from you. All kinds of things ran through my head."

Chris reached for her hand and squeezed. "It's okay. I understand. It was a lot of stress for one week, and I don't blame you."

Stress. He had no clue. "Steve showed up at my house earlier. Claimed he'd heard my pets were missing while talking to his friend at the Sheriff's Office and came to help me find them. Steve said terrible things about you."

He let go of her hand, and his forehead wrinkled. "But why? I don't know him."

"I demanded he leave, and then he—" Tears exploded in her eyes.

"He what?" Chris recaptured her hand. She grabbed his with her free hand. "Take a breath, Alanna."

"Steve pushed me into the house. He slammed the door shut. Started kissing me." Heat flooded her face. "I rammed my knee into him, and he let go. I ran out the back door."

Chris's brows furrowed, and his nostrils flared as he whispered, "Did you report him? He'd better not show up again."

The waitress placed their food in front of them.

He squeezed Alanna's hand. "Let's pray." Chris bowed his head. "Lord, before I ask You to bless this food, I'm asking that You'll do something with this Steve guy. Help the authorities deal with him and find out what happened to Susie and Marmalade. Father, we thank You for the food. Please bless it to our bodies and nourish us. Thank You for getting me back to Texas safely and for keeping Alanna safe. And, please protect Susie and Marmalade, wherever they are. Thank You for your mercy. In Jesus's name. Amen."

Alanna added her amen, and they started eating. She forked a minuscule portion of eggs into her mouth and forced herself to swallow.

"So what did the Sheriff's Department say about Steve? Mighty convenient. In the right place at the right time to hear of two missing pets?" Chris's eyes narrowed. "But why would he do it? To get rid of the animals so he could molest you? That's what he tried, right?"

She grimaced and closed her eyes. "Yes."

"You did report him, didn't you?"

"Who'd believe me? No one was around to witness it."

As he stroked her cheek, heat raced up her neck and bloomed in her face. She smiled.

Chris lowered his hand.

"Steve's jealous of you." Alanna bit her lower lip.

"Yeah," Chris tilted his head and gazed into her eyes, "he has reason to if you feel toward me the same way I do you." He lifted her chin with his finger.

"I think Steve knew they were your pets." She shook her head. "I believe he had alcohol on his breath. Maybe that's the reason he's doing these crazy things. When I told him the accusations were a pack of lies and ordered him to leave, he said I'd come crawling back to him. As if we'd ever been together. That's when he pushed me into the house and grabbed me."

Alanna took a deep breath and closed her eyes. She could feel his groping hands. The horrible smell of his breath. She opened her eyes.

Chris took her hands in his. "It's okay." He stared at her half-eaten meal. "You didn't eat much?"

"Guess I'm not hungry."

"Me neither." He pushed his half-eaten plate of food away. "Let's get those copies made. We'll stop at Harris County Sheriff's Department afterward to see if they know anything. And you'll tell them what Steve did."

She'd rather find out where he lived and pound the truth out of him.

❄ ❄

Chris stood by Alanna at the Sheriff's Office as she explained her suspicions regarding the intruder in her home. He laid his hand on her shoulder to steady her when she told the officer what Steve had tried to do that afternoon.

As they left the building, Chris pulled his mouth to the side. Not much assurance from the Sheriff's Department. Not much comfort to Alanna or him. But they had to let the authorities handle things.

Alanna sighed. "Will they find Susie and Marmalade?"

With his arm around her shoulders, they headed toward his car. "We can hope."

As they drove away, he reached for her hand. "This past week, I did get much sleep. I'll need some before I pass out. But what do you say to a late steak dinner tonight? Except for what I had at the diner, I've been eating hospital food since I left Houston." He laughed, hoping to brighten

Alanna's mood. "The food wasn't bad, but Bob's Steak House is calling my name." He glanced at her with a grin.

She gave him one of her gorgeous smiles. "Steak actually sounds good. What time?"

"It's four-twenty-three. I'll set the alarm for six."

"One hour isn't much sleep, and you've had a long drive. I can make dinner for you. Steaks can wait until tomorrow after we hang the rest of the flyers."

He kissed her knuckles. "I'll be fine. I've gone with far less sleep and more stress than this in the past."

"If you're sure."

"Oh, before I go anywhere, let's get each other's cell numbers in our phones."

Alanna giggled.

He pulled into the driveway, and they stored the phone numbers in their cells. Chris accompanied her inside the house. As they entered, all was quiet.

Chris checked the kitchen door and front rooms, while she went through the bedrooms.

"Everything's secure." He kissed her at the door and listened for her to throw the deadbolt before he left the porch.

After driving to his apartment, he took a shower and shaved. Chris set the alarm before getting into bed. What would Camaro guy try next? *The creep better not go back to Alanna's, or he'll have more than an angry knee to deal with.*

Chapter Sixteen

C hris slapped the alarm and rolled out of bed, then yawned and stretched. He forgot it would be so dark by the time the alarm went off. This would mess with his system tonight as far as sleeping, but hey, he'd be wide awake for his date with Alanna. He grinned and hurried to the bathroom to wash up.

He dressed in jeans and a light blue western shirt. Hope she liked the cowboy look. He grabbed his keys and jumped into the Malibu.

When Alanna answered the door, his mouth dropped open. Adrenaline rushed through him like rapids on a river. Her powder-blue sweater gently hugged her curves, and a Navy-blue skirt with matching shoes finished the picture of loveliness. He restrained his desire to caress her beautiful strawberry-blonde hair as it fell over her shoulders. Always did have a thing for strawberry-blondes. *Snap out of it, Maguire.*

After swallowing the lump in his throat, he blew a gentle whistle. "You look stunning. And—" He held his arms out to his sides. "We're color-coordinated." He laughed.

Her cheeks flushed as she chortled and opened the door wider for him to enter. "Let me grab my jacket."

The scent of jasmine filled his senses as he helped her put on her wrap, letting his hands linger on her shoulders longer than necessary. He wrestled with the urge to envelope her in his arms and just forget dinner. Where had this passion come from? How long had it laid dormant? She'd awakened a part of him he'd all but forgotten.

As they entered Bob's Steak House, the aroma of onions, garlic, and meat on the grill greeted them. His mouth watered. "I may have to order mine rare tonight." He glanced at her. "Won't take so long to cook."

Alanna tittered. "Easy, boy." She patted his arm. "Look at the beautiful Christmas tree they have. And so nostalgic with all those ornaments of things from days gone by."

"Really nice." Chris fingered a tiny red tractor. "This would be my favorite."

"I'm partial to the little milk cans, myself. But everything is perfect. Makes me miss my parents' farm."

The hostess interrupted and led them to a table. When they were seated, she handed them menus.

Chris gazed at Alanna. "You have the most gorgeous green eyes. Like polished emeralds sparkling with an inner light."

Color blossomed in her cheeks. "I thought you were hungry." She pointed to the menu.

He smiled. Loved the way she blushed. "But, I love your green eyes."

"Stop that. I'll bet you tell all your green-eyed patients the same thing, not to mention fiery-haired Becka at work."

He sat back and let his jaw drop. "You question my sincerity?" His head shook slowly. "First of all, I give such compliments only to patients over sixty, and secondly, I wouldn't dare say it to Becka. She'd box my ears. She's married, you know. I've met her husband. *And,* he'd box more than my ears if he found out."

Alanna laughed and covered her mouth.

"But hers can't compare to the iridescence in yours. They are beautiful. So are you."

The waiter approached the table and took their orders for steak and onion rings.

After the young man left, Chris turned to Alanna. "You know, in all the time we've spent together, I've never asked you where you go to church."

"I was attending the one Jake and I started going to right before he died, but it doesn't seem right anymore. I haven't been back for months."

"Would you like to join me tomorrow for morning service? I go to Stone Ridge Bible Church in the Woodlands community."

A smile spread across her face. "I'd enjoy that."

Joy filled him when she didn't hesitate. Now he knew for sure she was a believer. His heart thumped.

The waiter returned and placed their food in front of them. Chris slipped his hand under hers and asked the blessing.

While they ate, they made small talk about his trip to Florida and how he and Chet had met.

Alanna focused on the small piece of steak at the end of her fork. "What a blessing to have someone like that in your life. Faithful friends. The way you've been to each other." She continued the fork's journey to her mouth.

"Chet has been. And I had to be there for him. Again, I'm sorry I hadn't entered your number into my cell. I wanted to kick myself when I got to Chet's place." He bit into an onion ring.

Her green eyes captured his. "It's okay. And I'm sorry I entertained the thought that you'd take Susie and Marm. But we haven't known each other very long. I wasn't sure what to think."

"No. Not long at all." Chris leaned back and pushed the empty plate away.

Alanna placed her napkin on hers. "That was a perfect steak."

He straightened. "Let's go back to your house and pray for Susie and Marmalade and for the Sheriff's Department to find our kids."

She smiled. "Good idea." But the smile faded. "Do you really believe we'll get them back?"

Alanna filled the coffeemaker with water and measured the grounds. She started the machine and joined Chris in the living room.

As he reclined on the couch, he stared at the corner where Susie and Marmalade always curled together for a nap.

She sat beside him and placed a hand on his arm. "It's as if they'd grown up together in that corner of the sofa. They were here for such a short time, but it's strange not to see them there asleep." Tears burned her eyes, but she blinked them away.

Chris laid his hand over hers. "We'll get them back."

She leaned toward him and rested her head on his shoulder. "I hope so."

He shifted and faced her but said nothing. Taking both her hands in his, he bowed his head. "Father, we're coming to You for help. Susie and Marmalade are missing, and You know where they are. Please help us or the Sheriff's Department find them. And please protect them."

Chris paused and cleared his throat. "And Lord, thank You, especially for bringing Alanna into my life. I'm certain it was Your design for us to meet." He fell silent.

When he squeezed her hand, she peeked at him. His brows were pinched. Should she finish his prayer? "Lord, we love You." Did she? "And we'll trust in Your will for all this." Could she? "Thank You for bringing Chris home safely from Florida and for working things out for Chet and his dad. Amen."

Chris added a faint amen and raised his head. His eyes glistened as they locked onto hers. His thumb tenderly brushed her knuckles, and a lightning-bolt charge surged through her as if she'd touched a live wire. She couldn't draw her eyes away. *It's too soon. It's too soon for feelings like this.*

Alanna stood. "Let's have that coffee, and indulge in the strawberry cheesecake we brought home." *Home.* Maybe someday it would be the two of them at home, together.

His face brightened. "You have a way of getting to my heart, lady. Not that you haven't been there before." He chuckled.

All through dessert and afterward, the idea of going home to Ireland haunted Alanna. No need to go. Not since Chris was here...in her life.

Someday in the near future, she'd make a trip to see her ma and da and spend time with Meg and her family. But not now. What if Chris went with her? She'd better stop jumping ahead of herself...and him.

He reached for her hand. "With that emotional moment we had before I left, you had second thoughts about me while I was away, didn't you? Is that why you're so quiet? I don't blame you. I didn't handle any of it well. For a doctor, I sometimes don't have my act together."

"I doubt that's the case, Doctor Maguire." She grinned. "But, I have to admit, I was pretty upset. I even contemplated going home to Ireland...for a visit. That's when you found me crying on the back porch. I didn't know what to do or think."

"That's right. You did tell me you lived there before you met Jake. A real Irish colleen." He glanced at her. "And now? Still thinking of going?" He dropped his gaze to the cup in his hands. "I'd understand if you do, even though I don't want you to go. Not right now. But if you have to."

Could this man be any sweeter? *I am in love with him.* Alanna slid her arm around his back and rubbed his shoulder. "I don't plan to go to Ireland. Not anytime soon. If I do, it'll be in the future. After all, I have a new job and can't go traipsing off. I don't get vacation time until next year."

He stared at her. "So, you're worried you'd lose your job?"

She laughed. "Not entirely." Alanna dropped her head to his shoulder. "That's not it at all. It's more...I know everything's okay between you and me, so I don't want to leave." She lifted her eyes to meet his. "And I couldn't leave without knowing what's happened to Susie and Marm."

Their faces inched closer together. She held her breath. His lips claimed hers, warm and comforting. Jake's image slammed into her thoughts. *Stop, Alanna.* She pulled back and jumped to her feet. "I wish the Sheriff's Office would call and tell us something already."

Would she always feel she had betrayed Jake when she kissed Chris?

Chris glanced at his watch. Midnight. Where had the evening gone? After walking with Alanna to the front door, he fidgeted with his keychain. Alanna's mood had changed when he kissed her tonight. He wrapped her in his arms and leaned his back against the front door. Her arms traveled around his waist, resting her head on his chest.

Each time they were together, it grew harder to leave her. But he had to be patient. One question plagued him. Was she ready for a new commitment, or not? Her marriage hadn't been like his and Sheila's, one focused solely on love for their son instead of each other. Alanna and Jake had been true lovers and friends. She may never get over that. He couldn't read more than loneliness into her reactions. Not yet.

He raised his cheek from the top of her head and turned to open the door. Her hand grabbed his forearm. "Chris, is there any more we can do to find Susie and Marmalade? I feel so helpless."

"After church tomorrow, we'll do another search. We can stop for lunch and then come back here to see if, by chance, they've returned." He patted her hand. "And if not, we'll search through the neighborhood and move outward in concentric circles. They have to be somewhere."

Tears edged her eyes as she gazed up at him and nodded. He held her again and whispered, "I'd better go." When he lifted her chin and kissed her, soft lips melted on his. Her hand rose to his neck, and her fingers tickled him as they touched the back of his neck.

Chris backed away. *Lord, I need strength.* He'd put all his focus on finding the pets this weekend. Not allow any lulls in his and Alanna's conversations. Not sit too close to her for too long. And definitely not hold her.

Her brows knit, and she pressed her lips together. She must be struggling with conflicting emotions too. He couldn't take advantage and make things harder on her. No more kisses until she gave him a sign she was ready to commit to their relationship. It had to be the loneliness that made her respond to him the way she did.

Chris opened the door and smiled. "I'll pick you up at nine-thirty tomorrow for church. And don't worry. We *will* find Susie and Marmalade." *Lord, please, You have to let us find them.*

Chapter Seventeen

The following Friday evening, Chris strode up the walkway to Alanna's house, a dozen yellow roses in hand. As he sighed, his shoulders drooped. A whole week had passed with no news from the Sheriff's Department. Why hadn't they found out who broke into Alanna's house and took their pets? She told them who she suspected. He rang the doorbell and glanced at the picture window. Sure missed those *kids*.

Alanna opened the door, and he caught a whiff of roast beef. His salivary glands ignited, making him twice as hungry as he'd been before leaving his apartment. "What a tantalizing aroma." He shut his eyes and took in a second deep breath.

As he exhaled, he gazed at her. She was even more tempting. "What are you trying to do, make me feel like an old man with that bouncy ponytail?" He laughed. Man, she looked incredible in that purple sweater and faded jeans. His pulse rate increased.

Chris stepped back and made a show of checking the address next to the door frame. "Am I at the right house? I was looking for Alanna McCarthy, not a teenybopper."

She placed her hands on her shapely hips. Her mouth twisted. "Are you saying I'm underdressed for the occasion, Doctor Maguire? But look at you. You don't look much out of your teens in that Star Wars T-shirt and western jeans. Where'd you park your steed?"

They chuckled, and he entered the foyer. He loved the way they had become so relaxed with each other. Their bantering always tickled him. Chris closed his eyes again and savored the aroma of freshly baked bread.

He swung the bouquet of roses from behind his back and held it out to her. "Lady, you could wear overalls, hold a wrench, and be covered with oil from head to toe, and you'd be perfectly dressed in my eyes." He lowered his brows. "Maybe not the oil part."

Alanna giggled. She took the roses from his hand. "Thank you. They're beautiful." As she headed to the kitchen, she called over her shoulder, "Dinner is almost ready."

After lowering himself to the couch, Chris stretched his long legs out in front of him and gazed around the room. A couple of weeks 'til Christmas, but Alanna hadn't done any decorating, inside or out.

The lady strolled into the living room and sat next to him, a glass punch cup in her hand. "I made homemade eggnog. My mother's recipe. But you don't have to drink it if it's not your thing."

He took the cup from her hand and sipped. "This is good. Best I've ever tasted. Eggnog isn't my first choice for a beverage, but yours will be from now on."

"You don't have to say that. It's okay if you'd prefer something else. Cola, ginger ale, milk, bottled water—"

As he took another mouthful from the cup, his hand flew up to stop her. He picked up a napkin from the coffee table and wiped his mouth. "I'm not kidding. This is wonderful."

Her smile reached her eyes.

When he finished the drink, he placed the cup on the table and drew her to his side. His arms encircled her, and their lips met. He backed away an inch. "You taste better than the eggnog." His lips found hers, their sweetness igniting his passion. Skyrockets exploded in his head when she responded.

Alanna dropped her head back. "Chris." Her tone was breathy. She took in a deep gulp of air, broke away from his embrace, and rose from the couch. She tightened her ponytail. "We'd better eat dinner."

Whoa. "I think you're right." He needed to chill. Hadn't he told himself a week ago he wouldn't do this?

He followed her into the dining room. "Are you expecting royalty with all this china and crystal?" His chest tightened at the tall crystal vase with the roses he'd given her displayed in the middle of the table. "You really went all out."

She aimed another bright smile at him. "So did you with the roses. I've always loved to entertain, but I haven't done much for a long time." Alanna pulled out the chair at the end of the table. "You can sit here while I serve the food." She turned and left.

Avoiding the seat at the head of the table, he sat at the place setting on one side. Must be pure habit to pull out Jake's chair. At the kitchen table when they'd eaten together was one thing, but the dining room was a whole different story.

She returned, carrying a steaming bowl of mashed potatoes and set it on the table. "Chris, please sit here." She laid her hand on the back of the chair she'd pulled out. "The man should sit at the head of the table."

He rose from his seat. "I didn't want to presume." He moved to the chair she held onto. "Can I help you bring the food in?"

"Everything's under control. And you weren't presumptuous." She returned to the kitchen.

"Alanna, not to change the subject, but why haven't you decorated for Christmas? Don't you celebrate the holiday?"

She returned, pushing a small wooden kitchen cart that held a platter of roast beef and a bowl of green beans. Additional plates and bowls of food covered the second shelf, along with the loaf of baked bread in a basket.

"You are organized. I'll give you that."

She giggled. "What did you ask me?" She seated herself in the chair Chris had vacated.

"I wondered why you hadn't decorated for the holiday. The question won't make you sad, will it?"

"No. I haven't had a chance to bring the boxes down from the attic since I started the new job. With the trauma of the break-in, it's been too much to worry about Christmas decorations." She passed the meat platter to him. "I haven't sent my niece and nephew their presents either, and it'll take forever for them to get to Ireland, especially this near the holiday."

They filled their plates and bowed their heads. Chris gave the blessing.

He took a bite of the roast and rolled his eyes. "Mmm. You can't get roast beef this good in a restaurant. That's it! You can cook for me any day." He took a drink of eggnog. "I'm not making your head swell, am I? I like it the size it is." He laughed.

She shook her head. "I'll squeeze it back to shape tonight. But keep those compliments coming. A girl needs to know when she's appreciated."

After dinner, Chris helped load the dishwasher and then led her to the living room. "Alanna, may I help you decorate? I don't do anything at my apartment, mainly because I'm a guy, and I'm rarely there. But I love Christmas." He sat on one end of the couch.

"Hold that thought." She hurried back to the kitchen. A second later, she rolled in the coffee cart and took the armchair. "Decorating together would be fun." She poured their coffee. "Are you busy tomorrow?"

"Nope. Didn't plan anything except to ask if I could spend it with you. If your gifts for your sister's kids are ready to go, we can stop by the post office and take care of that. You can email and tell them the packages will arrive late. Kids don't care as long as they get presents."

"Ha! That's what my da always says."

He grinned. "Have you told your family about me?"

Alanna's heart thumped. "Thank you. I need you to keep me on the ball with all this holiday stuff." She dreaded calling her sister to explain what happened with her job, much less tell them a new man came into her life. It wasn't that she didn't want to tell her family, but she'd get such flak for waiting so long. Maybe she shouldn't mention him at all. Not after the lectures she got when she'd first met Jake. Alanna let out a long sigh.

She dished up the Dutch Apple Pie and sat back.

When they finished their dessert, Chris leaned back on the cushions. "You are one terrific cook." He stretched his legs out and yawned. "You didn't answer my question. Did you tell your folks about me?"

"Haven't had a chance to tell them yet, but I will." Change the subject. "It's been a long day. Not that I'm trying to get rid of you, but shouldn't you go home and get your rest? This was a frantic Friday at work, even if we did get off early. And you had that call from the hospital that made your day longer." It'd be a good idea for them not to spend too much time alone, doing nothing but being with each other, and— Heat spread through her neck. She needed to find things for them to do when he came over. Things to keep their minds and hands busy. Not to mention their lips. Tomorrow they'd decorate, and she could get out the board games she and Jake had accumulated.

"You're right. As much as I hate leaving, I have been up since four this morning. Besides, I have a date with a gorgeous blonde tomorrow, and I don't want to be too tired to enjoy it." He winked. "What time shall I show up?"

"The post office is open from nine to noon, so...would you like to come for breakfast? How do pancakes sound?"

Chris hopped up from the couch. "They're my favorite. Thank you. You're spoiling me, and I love it." He pulled her up from the chair.

Alanna followed him to the front door, and he threw on his jacket. When he turned to her, her heart wilted. Perhaps one day, there'd be no need for him to leave. Oh no! She'd done it again. Thoughts she shouldn't entertain at this point. She blinked the burning from her eyes.

Chris pulled her to him and kissed her gently.

Warmth and safety enveloped her in his arms. She never wanted him to leave. Not ever. Could he feel the longing she had for him?

A moment later, Chris stepped out the door and got into his car. Alanna watched from the front window as he disappeared into the night. She bolted the door and leaned back against it. Tomorrow would be another day to spend with this dream of a man.

As she turned on the dishwasher, concerns filled her mind. Would he get bored spending the entire day with her alone if they kept busy with other things besides kissing and—? If Susie and Marmalade were here, he'd have something else to keep his mind occupied. *That's silly.* They'd had fun times talking and enjoying each other's company. It was during those lulls in conversation or activity when their emotions intensified. *Don't put such thoughts in your head.*

What joy Chris, Susie, and Marm had brought into her life. *God, please bring our furry kids back. I can't bear to think of them out there in the cold. Or hurt. Please, Lord. You brought Chris back. Please bring Susie and Marmalade back too.*

Alanna turned off the kitchen light and ran to her bedroom. She fell onto the bed and let the tears flow. Would God listen to her after she'd been so doubtful of Him? Did Chris really believe they'd get them back?

Chapter Eighteen

hris hung the last of the garlands over the picture window and then stepped off the ladder. "It took us a few days to decorate your entire house and my apartment inside and out. And next week is Christmas. We can't celebrate without a tree." He hadn't decorated a tree in so long.

When the ladder shook, Alanna grabbed his arm. "The artificial tree's still in the attic. It's so big, I was tempted to buy a smaller one."

Chris folded the ladder, carried it to the kitchen, and leaned it on the wall near the back door. "Before I leave for the evening, I'll stow this in the shed. Here's an idea. Hopefully, a good one. You'll have to decide. Why don't I get a real tree for you? You have the ornament boxes piled in the dining room...next to the games you keep winning." He narrowed his eyes, then laughed. "Let me do the man-thing and find a fresh tree."

She chortled and nodded. "Okay, he-man. The job is yours." She pursed her lips. "You were afraid I'd ask you to crawl up in the attic and get that monster, weren't you?"

He placed his hand over his mouth. "Hee-hee-hee." Could he love this woman any more than he did right at this moment? Such a wit. "Not really. My folks always had a live tree. Dad and I would hunt until we found the perfect one and bring it home to Mom. We'd put it up and decorate it on Christmas Eve. Family tradition. It could be why I never decorate. I miss my folks since they passed."

She poured a cup of coffee and set it in front of him on the kitchen table. "I understand. I miss my folks in Ireland, hundreds of miles away."

After she'd poured a cup for herself, she sat opposite him.

He reached for her hand. "We'll celebrate the holiday together." Chris moved to the chair next to her and kissed her. "Shall we put the tree up on Christmas Eve?"

The doorbell rang, and she pulled away. Alanna rushed to the door and peered through the peephole. "It's Deputy Teague," she called to Chris.

As she swung the door open, Chris joined her in the foyer. "Please come in, Officer. Can we get you a hot cup of cocoa or coffee?"

"No, thank you." He shook Chris's hand and turned to Alanna. "I came by to let you know we've made an arrest in your break-in case. One of your neighbors, who at first didn't want to get involved, finally told us she had seen a person carry out two animal cages from your backyard the day of the crime."

"Was it Steve Brennan?"

The deputy nodded. "We couldn't arrest him on your hunch. Had no evidence since everything had been wiped clean. No fingerprints. But when we confronted him with the witness's statement, he confessed. He's been charged with breaking and entering."

"I knew it. I knew there was something fishy with him showing up the next day, knowing the animals were gone."

"Yes, ma'am. Dumb as it sounds, he claims he'd been drinking that day and came up with a hair-brained idea that if the animals went missing, he could help you find them."

Chris laid his hand on her shoulder. "Figured you'd be grateful enough to go out with him, I suppose."

Alanna grimaced. "Deputy, you look tired. Please, come in and have a seat."

"It's this cold weather. Wears me out. Strange for this part of Texas." He followed Chris and Alanna into the living room and sat on the armchair. "Miss, I seriously don't believe you need to worry about Brennan coming after you again. Turns out, he'd lost his job at the hospital and was depressed. That's why he'd been drinking. Says he wasn't thinking straight. Admitted to pushing his way in here, and being obsessed with you. But he said he'd never hurt you. He sounded apologetic and ashamed."

She shook her head and then riveted the officer with a stare. "But where did he take Susie and Marmalade?"

The officer shrugged. "All he remembers is driving for a long time and letting them out in the country somewhere. Sorry. He seemed repentant over what he did. Said he hopes we find them. And that you'll forgive him."

Alanna entered the kitchen while Chris continued to talk to the officer. She returned with a cup of cocoa and handed it to the deputy.

When she sank to the couch, Chris wrapped an arm around her. He whispered into her ear, "We'll find them. No matter how long it takes. We'll find them, sweetheart." He kissed her cheek.

Officer Teague smiled at him, finished his cocoa, said his goodbyes, and left.

When the door closed, Alanna burst into sobs. "What could have happened to Susie and Marmalade, Chris? It's so cold out there."

"God knows, and He'll take care of them for us." He cast a wary eye at the blustery wind outside. *Why haven't You let us find them, Lord?*

Chapter Nineteen

Alanna propped her wrapped Christmas gift for Chris in the corner of the living room where tonight he'd deliver and set up the tree. He'd love the painting she'd found for him. She'd been fortunate to find a picture with an orange cat next to a dog who looked similar to Susie. A parakeet on the pooch's head was a bonus. She giggled. He loved animals and birds. She should have asked Meg to paint one, but even if she had asked her sister, there wouldn't have been time to finish a painting and ship it for Christmas.

If only she could surprise him with the real pets. Would they ever be found? But at least she had Chris to celebrate with this year.

Alanna arranged the two gifts she'd wrapped for Susie and Marmalade beside Chris's. Was she crazy to hope they'd find those two little furbabies? Where might they be? Sure, they lived in Texas, but this year was freezing cold—they might— She couldn't finish the thought. A shiver sprinted down her spine, and tears pooled in her eyes.

She blinked them back and stood, glancing at her watch. Chris should be here any minute. Better check the ham.

Forty-five minutes later, Alanna paced the front room. Where was he? He hadn't answered his cell. Dinner was past ready. Wrapped in foil with the oven set on low, everything might not dry out, if he got here soon. "Why didn't he answer the phone?"

As she knelt on the couch and checked out the front window for the umpteenth time, her cell rang. She snatched it from the coffee table. "Chris, where are you? I called. Dinner's been ready for almost an hour. Is something wrong?"

"Honey, I'm sorry I'm late. But when I explain, I don't think you'll be too upset with me. And I didn't answer the cell because I was driving."

"What? You couldn't pull over?"

"Sweetheart, I can tell you're worried, but everything is okay. I'm pulling into the driveway and will explain everything in a few minutes. Do me a favor. Unlock the front door and go to the kitchen."

Go to the kitchen? "Why?" What was he up to?

"Please? For me?"

"Okay, but I don't understand." With the phone stuck to her ear, she headed out of the living room, through the dining room, and into the kitchen. She peeked through the doorway toward the front door. "I'm in the kitchen."

"Alanna...no peeking."

How did he know? She moved to the far end of the room. "I'm in the *back* of the kitchen."

"Promise you won't peek?"

She exhaled loudly. "I *promise*. Will you please get in here before dinner is ruined, and my anxiety consumes me? You're something else, mister."

"Nice to have someone worry about me, by the way." He chuckled and ended the call.

She laid the cell on the counter, tapped her foot on the kitchen floor, and folded her arms across her middle. The front door opened with its familiar squeak. Paws clattered across the foyer's wood floor. Alanna gasped, dropped her arms, and held her breath.

Susie and Marmalade, both adorned with bright red bows and brand new pink collars, burst into the kitchen. Alanna dropped to her knees and opened her arms wide. As Susie bounced against her, Alanna fell backward to the floor. She rolled to her side, her face instantly covered with slobbery kisses. Marmalade hopped onto Alanna's hip, purring her loudest, and pushed alternating front paws in and out as if kneading dough.

"Okay, okay, guys. I'm happy to see you too. Oh, so happy. Enough with the happy paws, Marmy." As she tried to stand, she lost control of her giggles.

Chris's face appeared around the corner. "Merry Christmas Eve."

Chris stifled a laugh, held out his hand, and helped Alanna to her feet. "Let me get the kids settled on the couch, and I'll give you a hand getting the food on the table. I'm sorry it took me so long to get here, but are you disappointed?"

Alanna planted a firm kiss on his cheek. "Does that answer your question, Doctor?"

Before she washed her hands, she grinned and gave each furbaby one more pat.

"Come on, kids, up on the cushions. Mom has work to do, and so do I. You get more to eat after we've had our dinner." He winked at the pets, and they ran to their favorite corner of the sofa.

Once the animals settled into their cuddle position, Chris reentered the kitchen and helped Alanna transfer the dinner to the dining room.

After Alanna took another look at Susie and Marmalade curled up together, she sat in her chair at the table. "It's so good to have them home. But, how?"

"You've got that right. I'll fill you in while we eat."

They filled their plates, and Chris asked the blessing.

Alanna leaned back, repositioned her arms across her stomach, and pinned Chris with a stare. "Spill the beans, mister. Who, what, where, when, and why...and most of all, *how?*"

He guffawed, took a bite of ham, and swallowed. "Here's the story. Last week, while I scoured the countryside for the best place to find a Christmas tree, a dog resembling Susie jumped out on the road ahead. I sped to the dirt road the dog had run down, but when I got there, the dog was nowhere in sight."

Alanna stopped eating, fixed on his every word.

Chris swallowed a forkful of candied yams. "I went to the farm at the end of that road and asked if they'd seen a dog and cat wandering around. The elderly couple living there, Rick and Faye Templar, said a dog and cat had shown up at their place around the first of the month." He waved his fork in a circle. "That was right when Steve had stolen Susie and Marmalade."

He took a drink of apple cider. "I figured Steve must have taken off their collars and let them out of the carriers on the road leading to the farm.

"Faye said she tried to coax them inside, but they ran to the barn instead. That night, her husband found them asleep inside, burrowed in a pile of hay."

"Why didn't you tell me?"

Chris pressed his lips together. He lowered his ham-laden fork. "I didn't want to give you false hope because the lady said they'd disappear each day and come back at night. The rascals wouldn't let the woman or her husband near them, so I wasn't positive it was Susie and Marmalade."

He forked a bite of food into his mouth and pointed to her plate. "Come on. Don't let your food get cold. Everything's all right now."

Alanna raised her fork and ate a piece of fried apple without taking her eyes off him.

He smiled. "When I showed Faye our kids' picture, she thought the dog and cat staying in the barn might be our pets. She'd taken food and water out to the barn each morning, but they were always gone by then. Rick made sure they were back inside the barn before he closed the doors each night. They were usually eating the food his wife had left for them. He couldn't say for certain the dog and cat were our pets either. So I decided to not say anything to you until I knew."

Chris heaped mashed potatoes on his fork. "I went out to the farm whenever I could, hoping to catch them."

"When did you find them?"

"I'm getting to that. On my third trip, I found out the couple sold cut-your-own Christmas trees." He grinned. "I picked one out, Rick marked it sold, and he held it for me to pick up today. When I arrived this morning, he cut it down and tied it up for me."

Chris took another bite of food. "By the way, I pitched the tree over the fence into the backyard right before we came in."

"Never mind the tree. Were Susie and Marmalade there? Get to that part."

"Okay, okay. No. they weren't there. We loaded the tree on the roof of the car. The couple wished me good fortune and merry Christmas. The missus told me to come back as often as I'd like to look for the animals. As I left, I decided to drive around the area before I returned to town. One last-ditch effort to check for the dog and cat."

With his fork, he folded an asparagus spear in half and stuffed it into his mouth, then chewed for a few seconds. He washed it down with another drink.

Alana dropped her fork to the plate with a clatter and seized his wrist, forcing the bite of ham he'd stabbed to his plate. "Chris, I know you're hungry, but I'm dying to find out what happened."

If she wouldn't eat, neither would he. He'd better finish the story before their dinner was spoiled. He rested his utensil on the plate and folded his hands. "I headed down another dirt road that led to a field. A few yards in front of me, Susie popped out from the tall weeds on the side of the road. I slammed on the brakes, got out, and called her. She came right to me. But what a mess. Covered in hay, and from the smell, I could only imagine what else."

"But what about Marm?" Alanna's brow wrinkled, and she bit her lip despite the fact the pets were asleep on the couch. She flattened her hand between them on the table.

Chris enclosed her hand in his. "I asked Susie the same thing." He snickered. "She headed down the road, and I followed. When she trotted up to what looked like an old outhouse on the side of the field, a faint mew came from inside. The door must have slammed shut and stuck. I yanked on it, and out jumped Marmalade."

"But still, you didn't call me." Her eyes misted.

"I was going to. But I decided to surprise you instead." He furrowed his brows. "They needed to be cleaned up first, *really* cleaned up. Both of them carried the distinct aroma of barn. Or maybe outhouse." He wrinkled his nose. "They hopped right into the back seat of my car." Chris rolled his eyes.

"I drove back to the farm to tell the couple I'd found them. They were delighted. They were also glad the animals belonged to us, though they said they would have continued to take care of them."

Alanna blew a breath between her lips and glanced at the pets napping in the living room. She smiled.

"A strange thing happened before I took off. Rick reached his hand through the cracked-open back window, and Susie allowed him to pet her. He said it was the first time she'd let him touch her. So his wife stuck her hand into the back seat on the other side of the car. Marmalade stood on her back legs at the window, purred like crazy, and let the woman scratch her ears. Rick said, 'Don't that beat all?'

"I figured Susie and Marmalade sensed we'd find them eventually, and our kids didn't want this couple to get attached to them. It's the only thing that made any sense." Chris shook his head. "The kids and I left with an open invitation from the Templars for all of us to visit the farm any time."

After a long sigh, Alanna pressed her left hand to her heart. She picked up her fork and began to eat.

Good. She'd finally relaxed. "When I got the kids home, I fed them and gave each a thorough washing. Not the easiest thing to do with a cat, mind you. But she didn't give me too much of a fuss. Then we got ready to come here and surprise you."

Alanna rose, threw her arms around him, and wept. "This is the best Christmas present ever."

As he pulled her into his arms, adrenaline rushed through him. Just maybe, he could top it.

Chapter Twenty

Alana returned to her seat at the table and picked up her fork. Could Christmas get any better? "It's a miracle, having Susie and Marm back. Susie seems a bit chunky and tired. I'll make an appointment with the vet next week. Hope she's not sick."

"They looked fine to me, although I didn't do a thorough examination since I'm not a veterinarian. The vet appointment is probably a good idea for both of them." He lifted his fork. "Let's finish this excellent meal you made. We have to get the tree up and decorated. Tonight's a night for presents, and I see some in the corner of the living room." He shoved a forkful of meat topped with potatoes and peas in his mouth. His brows wiggled up and down.

After dinner, Alanna and Chris decorated the Christmas tree, the scent of pine filling the room. Susie made a point of sniffing each ornament as it was taken out of the box, and Marmalade batted at the few hanging from the lower branches.

Alanna turned off the lights in the room, and Chris switched on the tree lights. They stepped back to admire their work.

When she turned to leave the room and make coffee, Susie and Marmalade hopped back up on the cushions for another nap. Alanna spun and thrust her hands onto her hips. "You two are being lazy. Must be from all that fresh air at the farm."

Chris laughed and sat on the sofa next to them. "They ran around with cows, chickens, and horses, not to mention a few goats. But they're content to be home on this nice cushy couch with Mom and Dad."

Alanna chortled as she left the room. Her heart nearly burst to think of her and Chris being Mom and Dad to two four-legged kids. Would she ever get the chance to have the two-legged kind?

When the coffee was ready, she placed the decanter and the Baked Alaska she'd made on a cart and wheeled it into the living room. She placed the dessert on the table in front of the sofa.

"Alanna! Look out the front window."

As he drew the sheers aside, she kneeled on the cushions. She couldn't believe her eyes. Huge white flakes floated down from the sky. "Snow?"

He grinned, showing those perfect, pearly-white teeth and the irresistible dimple in his right cheek. "Snow! Now, it's Christmas Eve."

"Yes. But we're in Texas! *Houston,* Texas." She shook her head and reveled in the scene. The flakes glittered as they glided past the streetlight to the ground. Visions of Christmas in her childhood home drifted through her mind. "I'll bet it's snowing in Ireland too."

From behind her, Chris wrapped his arms around her shoulders. "Shall we fly over and see?"

She smiled and stood. "Some other time, perhaps." She turned to face him and gasped at the desire welling up inside her. When his hands touched her arms, an electrical charge raced upward and straight into her heart. "We'd better have our dessert—the Baked Alaska—on the table." Before she lost control. She pointed to the glistening meringue dessert.

He pressed his lips together, dropped his hands to his side, and turned in the direction she pointed. "I can't believe you made your own Baked Alaska." He took a couple of steps backward, then quickly sat down in front of the coffee table.

She exhaled. "Wasn't hard, once I found the recipe online. The hardest part was making the meringue." We'd better play some board games right after dessert. She cut into the mound on the platter and dished two slices onto the plates. "Now for the pièce de résistance." She ladled chocolate syrup over each piece and added forks.

"Lady, if you keep this up, I'll be as round as I am tall." He snickered.

She might just burst with happiness, overactive emotions, or not.

Chris devoured every crumb on his plate. He carried the dessert back to the kitchen, and Alanna followed, carrying the dirty dishes. She wrapped the rest of the dessert and tucked it into the freezer.

When she turned around, he took her hands in his. "May we ple-e-ease open presents? That'll keep me out of trouble." He winked at her.

The goofy grin on his face made her laugh. "I want you to open yours first."

"Sounds good to me." He kissed her forehead, spun, and all but dragged her into the living room. "The kids can have their presents when they decide to join the party. They're under the tree with yours."

Alanna stifled a giggle. She loved the little-boy, wide-eyed expression he sent her way. "Yours is the big one."

"As a kid, mine was always the biggest, being an only child." Chris brought the gifts back to the sofa and placed Susie's and Marmalade's next to them. They didn't budge. "They're sound asleep." He shrugged. "They can open theirs later. What do you say we take these out on the front porch and open them so we can enjoy the snowfall?"

He snatched their jackets from the coat tree, helped her put hers on, and followed behind her.

She opened the door and stepped out onto the porch. "Chris, I don't think I could get any happier than I am right now."

Chris tucked his gift for Alanna into his pocket before he joined her on the swing and stifled a chuckle.

Alanna threw a gray faux fur throw over their legs to keep them warm and snuggled next to him.

He glanced upward. "The snow's stopped, and the sky is clear. But it left enough white stuff to carpet everything. Beautiful." He pointed to the stars. "Look."

She leaned back on his shoulder. "Absolutely gorgeous. The sky's like a black velvet cloth with diamonds strewn across it, glittering from a jeweler's fluorescent light."

Her face glowed as though she hadn't a care in the world. Happy beyond words, he laid his cheek against her hair. "And the moon's sending beams through the tree, shafts of frost across the landscape." He pulled her closer. "It's a flawless night, sweetheart." She deserved a perfect night. He hoped she'd always remember it this way.

Alanna sat upright. "It's a lovely night, Chris." She reached for the large package she'd carried out. "Okay, you first, honey." She picked up the gift and handed it to him.

He cocked his head, his gaze locked on hers. "That's the first time you've called me anything other than Chris or Doctor. Sounds good." He ripped into the red wrapping paper and held the painting out in front of him. "This is great. Almost an exact match for Susie and Marmalade."

"Thought you'd like it for the bare wall in your office."

"It's terrific."

He lifted the small box out of his pocket. "Your turn."

Her brows pinched as her jaw dropped open. He placed the box in her hand, and she carefully opened it. Her eyes widened when she saw the sparkling ring. "*Chris.*"

"Alanna, our courtship has been a little unusual and in the fast lane..." he lowered himself to one knee, "and we can take as much time as you'd like. But I want you to be my wife in the not-too-distant future. I love you. Will you marry me?"

Her arms flew around his neck. Her lips searched and found his.

"Is this a yes?"

"Most definitely, a yes," she mumbled into his shoulder. "You've melted the icicles I've had in my heart for so long and replaced them with shining moonbeams. I love you too, Chris."

When she let go, he placed the sparkling one-carat diamond ring on her finger and pulled her back into his arms. She trembled.

"You're cold."

"No. Excited. And...it occurred to me...I'll *have* to tell my family about you now. Oh, Meg is going to kill me for waiting." She bit her lip.

"Still, we should go in. Can't have you getting sick." They stood. "And don't worry. Your family will love me, 'cuz you know how charming I am." He wiggled his brows at her. "I'll win them over in no time."

Alanna giggled again and hugged him around his middle.

After they'd hung up their jackets, he held her at arm's length. "This is such a happy night. I wasn't sure you'd say yes. The thought crossed my mind that you might not be ready to love another man yet."

"I wasn't sure I was...until you were late for dinner tonight. I couldn't bear the idea that something might have happened to you. Christopher McGuire, I promise to love you with all my heart."

"And I you." He brushed a strand of her long, strawberry-blonde hair away from her face. "Along with the other *kids* we'll have. The two-legged kind, I mean. Someday soon."

Her cheeks bloomed with color, and she buried her face in his chest. "Hopefully, very soon."

When they entered the living room, the corner of the couch where Susie and Marmalade had been sleeping was empty.

Alanna stared at him wide-eyed. "Where'd they go?"

Chris shrugged. He searched the living room and dining area while she ran down the hallway to the bedrooms calling for them. As she returned to the living room with worry written on her face, Chris spotted Marmalade running from the kitchen straight for them. Distressed moans came from the back of the house.

"Susie?" Alanna clamped onto Chris's arm. "Now, what's happened?"

Marmalade ran back to the kitchen, Chris and Alanna right behind her. They found Susie on her side in the bed she and Marmalade shared under the kitchen desk. Susie had delivered one puppy and was cleaning it. But a moment later, she shuddered and groaned in pain.

Alanna knelt at Susie's side, and in moments a second newborn pup appeared.

As Chris watched, she assisted the dog to deliver four more puppies. His jaw dropped open. "Lady, you amaze me. Where did you learn that?"

She shook her head and chortled. "I guess from living on my parents' farm. A natural response. We often helped the animals in their birthing. Susie was obviously in more pain than normal and needed a hand." She rocked back on her feet and stood. "Be right back."

After Alanna had cleaned up, Chris stepped behind her in the doorway between the kitchen and dining room with his arms around her. Susie lay on her side with her brood. Marmalade helped nudge each pup to its mother for nourishment and then sat outside the bed, keeping an eye on her canine nieces and nephews.

Chris's chin rested on Alanna's head. "Each of them looks exactly like a tiny Susie, except for the solid dark brown pup, the runt of the litter." He pointed to the squirmy runt in the middle of the group. "I can guess who the papa is." He tilted his head and glanced at Alanna. "My neighbor has a dog who resembles Susie, except he's chocolate brown.

"The owner says, his pet has learned to pull on the lever and open the front door when they forget to engage the deadbolt. So, he often runs loose in the apartment complex."

Alanna burst into laughter. "More Christmas Eve blessings. That's what they are."

He tightened his hold on her and smiled. "This must be a sign. We have a family to take care of. Maybe we should plan our wedding sooner rather than later, so we can make our own contributions right away."

She nodded with glowing cheeks. "I'll have to place that call to my family *right away* too. Meg will want to help plan the wedding. What a pain." She bit her lip and peeked up at him. "But marrying you, Doctor Maguire, will be well worth it."

He peered upward. "Mistletoe."

With a tilt of the head, Alanna narrowed her eyes. "Not that you've needed it before as an incentive."

He spun her around and pulled her tightly to him. "Nor do I now...or ever will in the future." His right cheek produced its dimple, and he winked.

Their lips met in a sweet, long, warm kiss.

Sharon K Connell

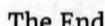

The End

About The Author

Raised in Illinois, Sharon K Connell went to school through college in Chicago for the most part. She also lived in Missouri, California, Florida, and Ohio. Her travels have taken her to all but six states in the United States, and she has visited Canada and Mexico. She is now a resident of Texas.

Sharon is a member of the American Christian Fiction Writers organization, Houston Writers Guild, 2 Elizabeths Literary Magazine, CyFair Writers, and the Christian Womens Writers Club (CWW). She runs the Facebook Christian Writers and Readers Group Forum and puts out Novel Thoughts, a monthly newsletter for writers as well as readers.

She is a graduate of the Pensacola Bible Institute in Florida and holds a certificate in fiction writing from the International Writing Program through the University of Iowa.

Her stories are about people whose life experiences turn them to God and increase their faith. Short stories she has written are in a variety of genres, but her primary genre is Christian Romance Suspense.

Let the words of my mouth, and the meditation of my heart, be acceptable in thy sight, O Lord, my strength, and my redeemer.
Psalm 19:14

Links

Website: https://www.authorsharonkconnell.com/

Amazon Author Page: http://www.amazon.com/author/sharonkconnell

Books page on Facebook:
https://www.facebook.com/averypresenthelpbook1

Author's Page on Facebook:
https://www.facebook.com/ChristianRomanceSuspense/

Group Forum on Facebook:
https://www.facebook.com/groups/ChristianWritersAndReadersGroupForum/

Twitter: https://twitter.com/SharonKConnell

Goodreads: https://www.goodreads.com/SharonKConnell

LinkedIn: https://www.linkedin.com/in/sharonkconnell

Pinterest: https://www.pinterest.com/rosecastle1/

AllAuthor: https://allauthor.com/search-page.php?q=Sharon+K+Connell

Other Works
by Sharon K Connell

A Very Present Help
Paths of Righteousness
There Abideth Hope
His Perfect Love

~

Short Stories in Anthologies

Ding-A-Ling Holiday Blues
in
Tales of Texas, Vol. 2

Spirit Lake
in
Dark Visions

Thank you for Reading

www.ingramcontent.com/pod-product-compliance
Lightning Source LLC
Chambersburg PA
CBHW022031170626
46808CB00003B/1143